THE BOOK OF MISUNDERSTANDINGS

by Robert Wexelblatt

Moon Rabbit Books & Ephemera

Lawrence, Kansas

2025

First published in 2025 by

Moon Rabbit Books & Ephemera

a wholly-owned subsidiary of

The Moon Rabbit Drinking Club & Benevolence Society

www.moonrabbitbooks.com

PO Box 3 / Lawrence, Kansas 66044 / U.S.A.

Library of Congress Control Number: 2025913011
ISBN 978-1-7348930-3-8 (print); 978-1-7348930-4-5 (epub)

Designed by
Patrick Giroux and Jay Holley

Illustrated by
Jay Holley

Miscellaneous refinements courtesy of
Stuart Bays

21 20 19 18 17 16 15 14 12 11 10 9 8 7 6 5 4 3 2

First Edition

Acknowledgments

"A Funeral," "At the Office," "A Coup de Théâtre," "Refugee in Riverside," "Izels," "Yezhovschina," "Politics," "The New Dentist," and "Failed State" first appeared in *Johnny America*

"Scott and Oswald" first appeared in *Shift*

"The Memory Unit" first appeared in *Blue Lake Review*

"Surprising Consequences of Our Revolution" first appeared in *Big Windows Review*

"Pretending is Pretending to Pretend" first appeared in *Corner Club Quarterly*

"The Theoretical Ship" first appeared in *Kennings Artistic and Literary Journal*

"The End of The War" first appeared in *Cleaver Magazine*

"Haran" first appeared in *Cake*

"Forgotten Actress" and "Grandfather's Dao" first appeared in *BlazeVOX*

"Kims and Parks" first appeared in *Offcourse Literary Journal*

"Report to the Society" and "A Most Unpleasant Story" first appeared in *Modern Literature*

Table of Contents

A Funeral

The day was a perfectly gloomy November Saturday, dark, damp, and chilly. Vogel, a professor of music who had lived alone since his long-ago divorce, dreaded the prospect before him but dutifully took the Brooks Brothers bag out of his closet and extracted the navy-blue suit in which he had been married. It still fit and did service for weddings and funerals. He no longer thought of the irony that the rituals of joy and grief should call for the identical uniform. He did reflect that, over the decades, funerals had come to outnumber weddings.

Dean's only one letter away from dead. That's what Vogel had replied when asked if he'd be a candidate the last time the job opened. Now the man who took on the position had died, and Vogel recalled his glib crack with some shame. A heart attack took the dean on Wednesday night. Friday brought an obituary in the University's daily with all the conventional commendations, chiefly from other deans, plus the Provost and President, but only a couple from faculty, and none at all from students. To Vogel, all administrators were guilty until proven innocent. He pretended not to have received the mass email asking him to eulogize the dean, a decent teacher of viola who had, in his view, gone over to the Dark Side. He and the deceased were not what could be called *simpatico*. Early on, they had argued about a new hire which rather iced their relationship. Their last conversation had been at the annual alumni reception. Vogel had talked, ostensibly with good humor, about the importance of administrators. The dean had just delivered a self-congratulatory speech larded with what he called "metrics": money raised, buildings refurbished, rankings elevated. Administrators love numbers. *Metrics* was almost the dean's favorite word. Vogel had once joked to a colleague that perhaps he would begin filing his annual reports in iambic tetrameter. After the speech, Vogel and the dean found themselves together near the bar. Vogel was starting on a second gin-and-tonic and, provoked by the dean's address, observed that the height of their office's ceilings and salaries were compensation for the knowledge that, though they believed themselves to be proprietors, administrators were, in fact, parasites. The dean affected to chuckle, but it was clear he was offended.

"Oh, come now. Really? *Parasites*?"

"Useful ones but, yes, parasites. And I can prove it."

The dean grimaced, looked longingly across the room, then snarled. "Okay, prove it."

"Well, it's simple. Imagine there are administrators like you but no faculty like me—and no students. Would the place still be a university?"

The dean frowned and emitted something between a chortle and a growl. Vogel pressed on.

"Now suppose there are faculty and students but no administrators. Of course, the place would be a shambles, a chaos. But it would still be a university, wouldn't it?"

They both laughed, not at all convivially, and the dean excused himself. Now that the dean had suddenly died, Vogel felt regret at the memory. It was one of the reasons he felt obliged to attend the dean's funeral and, if it couldn't be avoided, say something appropriate to his widow and children—he thought there might be two of the latter. He knew he had to pay his respects; moreover, he knew he ought to be seen paying them.

The funeral was at the Presbyterian church, 2 p.m., reception to follow. Vogel, not a churchgoer, looked up the directions on Google Maps. A lifelong fear of being late for a class or a concert had made Vogel almost pathologically punctual. The drive took less time than Google estimated, and he arrived at 1:35.

The stone church was square, solid, plain, and bluff, with red double doors. Its musty smell took Vogel back to the Sunday mornings of his childhood when the prayers were tedious, and even the shorter sermons felt interminable. He had yearned to be outside, beyond the stained glass, on his bike, playing ball. But he had liked the music and saw that the church had a small loft that was filled by an electronic organ with no room for a choir. He also spied an old spinet in a corner to the left of the pulpit.

About fifteen people were already there. A few were seated but most were clumped at the front, chatting in subdued voices. He recognized no one. He had met the dean's wife only once. She was, he thought, an anesthesiologist or pediatrician, and didn't attend academic events. If she and the dean gave dinner parties, he wouldn't have been invited. If he had ever seen the dean's children—two? three?—it would have been long before they grew up. Would the provost or president attend? It was possible, but Vogel doubted it.

More mourners arrived, the men dressed as he was; the women

wore hats and dark dresses. He didn't spot any of his colleagues. Who were these people?

An expensive casket, dark wood, highly polished, with bright brass fittings, was set up below the pulpit. It was open, but nobody went near it.

Vogel had a sudden misgiving. He took out and unfolded the notepaper on which he'd written the directions. *Presbyterian Church, 2 p.m.* He'd assumed there was only one Presbyterian Church, the First. He picked up a hymnal, looked inside the cover. *Property of Second Presbyterian Church.*

At that moment, a woman at the front of the church turned and stared at Vogel. Then she ran up the aisle, already in tears.

"You came!" she cried, seizing the hand without the hymnal.

Two more people, a young man and a young woman, made their way up the aisle.

The woman, still clasping Vogel's hand was clearly moved and she spoke rapidly.

"It was the last thing he said, his *dying words*, that he wanted to make it up with you, that he had to apologize for his bullying, for cheating you over the business, for shutting you out, for being such a bad brother. You got my letter? I wasn't sure of the address and, when you didn't answer or come to the hospital—" Here, she paused and turned to the two others, evidently the children. Vogel tried to object but she went right on.

"It's your Uncle Harold. He's come!"

"There's been a mistake," Vogel started again; but the widow, threw her arms around him, said she understood why he had every right to ignore her letter, but it meant so much that he was here now. The children looked at Vogel intensely and smiled. They too were eager to talk.

"I've wondered about you my *whole* life," said the young woman with real feeling. "The only picture we had was of Dad and you when you were kids."

"You look a lot like him," said the young man. "It's really amazing you're here. It means so much to Mom—to us, too."

"He blamed himself terribly, especially toward the end," the widow babbled. "It was prostate cancer, Harold, months of the most terrible pain, and, toward the end, when he was just skin and bones, all he talked about was you and wanting morphine. The physical suffering was awful, but his remorse was even worse. He *loved* you, Harold. He loved you and it was killing him that he couldn't apologize, that he couldn't see you and beg forgiveness and say goodbye."

Vogel hesitated. Such intense relief beside such pain was stunning. He made a decision that surprised him. He decided to say nothing.

The organist struck up the first chords of "Abide with Me."

"Come," said the widow, pulling his arm. "Come up front. You have to sit with us, the family."

Vogel went with them to the first pew. The widow sat to his right, the daughter to the left. He listened to the minister's eulogy and discovered that the dead man was named George and had lived an ordinary life, a bourgeois one. He played golf. He had a lot of friends. He had been a fair boss and ran the family Chevrolet dealership honestly—the business half of which Vogel surmised ought to have gone to his brother Harold. George had been active in the Rotary, a supporter of the church, enjoyed family vacations in national parks when the children were little, sponsored a Little League team, was a pillar of the community, loving husband, devoted father, and so on. Through it all, the widow held Vogel's hand tightly and wouldn't let go.

A golf buddy spoke briefly, also the dealership's sales manager, then the minister, but no one else.

The organist started a quiet rendition of a hymn Vogel recognized: "God Our Help in Ages Past."

Vogel rose with the others. The casket was right in front of them. The family approached it for the final farewell, the widow going first. She leaned down and whispered something. Then the children stood together. The daughter wiped at a tear and her brother put his arm around her waist. Then the three of them looked toward Vogel, smiling, nodding. He stepped forward and looked down at the face of the dead man. The funeral home must have worked hard to make him look so healthy, with suspiciously full cheeks and lips just shy of rosy.

Vogel looked down at the face of the dead man. He looked closely. There really wasn't any resemblance; yet Vogel felt strangely moved. He leaned down and kissed the corpse's cold forehead and, as he looked up, spotted the spinet. He went over to it, and everybody hushed, including the organist. He sat, opened the lid, looked over his shoulder at the widow, then began. He played the first two minutes of a piece of Bach's.

When he stood up, everyone was staring at him, some with surprise but others almost with reverence.

The widow rushed to his side, put her hand on his arm, her head on his shoulder. She was weeping.

"Oh, Harold. That was *so* lovely. George never mentioned that you played. What was that beautiful music?"

"A capriccio by Bach. It's called 'On the Departure of a Beloved Brother.'"

Hearing the title, the widow nearly collapsed from excess of feeling. Vogel supported her until the son and daughter took over.

After that, the four of them lined up beside the coffin to receive the mourners who had also queued and came forward, two-by-two. There was much hugging and condoling until the formality dissolved in a general milling about. That was when Vogel made his escape, when he took his departure.

At the Office

After the meeting during which A., an electrical engineer, presented her detailed plan for the company's next initiative, she overheard a product manager, B., in the corridor ridiculing a proposal and assumed he was deriding hers whereas, in fact, it was a hare-brained notion the industrial chemist C. had come up with over drinks the night before, and which, of course, had not been mentioned at the meeting. B. thought A.'s innovative idea remarkably good, but he did not speak up during the meeting because he was unqualified to assess its technical aspects but still more because he was attracted to A. and did not wish to appear to be ingratiating himself.

When they ran into each other in the cafeteria the next day, and B. began to compliment her, A. thought he was mocking her and gave him short shrift. After that, whenever B. addressed her, A. either pretended not hear him or replied curtly. Meanwhile, A. took every opportunity to denigrate B. to their colleagues. When he was told what A. was saying to others about him—such things are sure to make the rounds—B. was taken aback but reluctantly concluded that A. had conceived an antipathy for him; and, because the presentation which he had found so admirable had won her the ear of the higher-ups, she was in a position to do him harm, perhaps even get him dismissed. B. resolved to take measures to protect himself.

In this way, a genuine enmity grew up between A. and B. who, but for an unfortunate misapprehension, might, given that they were both young, unattached, and good-looking, have discovered that they were fond of Asian cuisine, skiing, large dogs, Russian novels, and French cabaret music; they could have started dating, become a couple, might have married, had children, supported one another in their careers, faced the vicissitudes of life together, and lived contentedly together for decades. Instead, their animosity grew to such a degree that they not only disparaged one another but recruited allies, establishing factions, and generated so much discord in the firm that, notwithstanding their excellent qualities, worthy contributions, and promising futures, their work and that of others suffered and, for the sake of amity and productivity, management finally determined that the best thing would be to let them both go.

A Coup de Théâtre

The audience in Rheinach Theater was growing restive when, midway through the premiere of the biographical drama, *Kafka and Girls* by the controversial playwright Hans Pinscher, Minnie Klugsuss forgot her lines. Her mind went blank, and, for a moment, she gaped at the male lead, Marek Bezdek, then said, "Another seven-and-seven, Herr Schaftsmann?" The sentence was a whimsy devised by her late father, something to say whenever she wished him to stop lecturing or making fun of her. It just popped into her head and she said it.

The audience stirred uneasily, but Marek didn't miss a beat.

"How about making it a seven-and-six? I'm feeling a little light-headed."

Minnie went with it. She raised a finger and replied, "Better be careful. If your head grows too light, those ears of yours might fly off with it."

Marek made an anxious face. "It's not impossible. My head could ascend into the ice mountains."

"How about just two ice cubes, then?"

Marek pretended to look even more worried. "It could ascend into the ice mountains and be lost forever."

"Accused men are all attractive, but you are also witty."

"Wit is for virtuosos. Virtuosity may be fit for preening lawyers, but for accused men it's out of place."

"But aren't *you* a lawyer?"

"Alas, yes. That will no doubt be another charge in the indictment."

"Then you've seen the charges?"

"Not as yet, but I have filed the necessary application along with the required affidavit and accompanying brief."

"I read somewhere that a lawyer is somebody who composes a document of ten thousand words and calls it a brief."

"My memory isn't perfectly reliable, but I believe I wrote that. A poor joke. But I admit, my brief isn't brief."

"See? Accused men are not only attractive and occasionally witty but also humble. I think that without much effort you could raise self-deprecation to a high art."

"Like a whining Klezmer clarinetist?"

"Not a bad analogy. So, would you like to have that drink now?"

Marek raised his arms and looked at her greedily. "I'd sooner have *you*."

Minnie took a step backwards and batted her eyelashes. "Maybe, but not yet. First, you must tell me what you like about me."

"Your fingers and your accessibility."

"Oh? And what do I remind you of?"

"A bridge. A bridge with long fingers and dependable legs."

Minnie laughed. "A bridge to what?"

"To the world understood by animals."

"By animals? Is that why the war between the sexes always ends in bed?"

Marek replied sententiously. "A perpetual war requires an infinite number of truces."

And so it continued, with Minnie and Marek improvising tenderly, angrily, gnomically, wittily, flirtingly until the performance did, indeed, wind up in bed.

The audience, of course, believed it was Pinscher's play. They began to find it interesting, then fascinating. The critics from the *Berliner Zeitung, Tagblatt,* and *Morgen-Zeitung* did too. All three noted that, while the play began ploddingly, it became electrifying halfway through. They all wrote glowing reviews. Demand for tickets soared; but, as the performance could hardly be repeated, the play closed.

Hans Pinscher was enraged. He hired a lawyer and sued the theater, the director, and especially Bezdek and Klugsuss. The brief came to just under ten thousand words.

A Coup de Théâtre

Refugee in Riverside

"Your great-grandfather was a tram driver. Professionally, he stayed on the rails, but at home he went off them once a month. This was down to his homemade slivovitz, which, for your information, is an infernal brandy made by fermenting plums."

Ten-year-old Stephen rolled his eyes at his brother Will, who shook his head. Always the same joke about the rails, always the hellish slivovitz. Still in their pajamas, they were seated on the sagging couch in their grandfather's living room on the morning of December 27. The lights on the tree were off; the room was chilly and full of shadows. At twelve, Will understood that the old man felt some compulsion to tell them the story of his life. He was willing to sit through it because he knew that his mother, for whom he would do anything, worried about her father. It was after their grandmother's death that she insisted they spend two days of Christmas week in their grandfather's drafty Victorian house. The boys went, Stephen stoically, Will under protest. Both would have preferred to be at home with their own beds, bathroom, presents, and friends.

By now, listening to their Djed's story was a seasonal ritual, like productions of *The Nutcracker* and *A Christmas Carol*. This was their third year. The old man was settled in his recliner with a mug of tea with honey. The boys sat still on the couch, doing their duty while their parents were upstairs sleeping—or pretending to.

"The alcohol made Otac crazy angry. Majka insisted that he was only blowing off steam, letting out all his dissatisfactions and disappointments, the bad memories from the war. He was usually a gentle man, my Otac. It was only when things went badly that he got into the slivovitz. Something went badly every month. But it wasn't so bad because by the time he came after us, the brandy spoiled his aim and his balance and, anyway, he soon passed out. All the same, I promised myself never to drive a tram or drink fermented plums. You understand? I was ambitious for another life, boys, a better one. I studied hard, as I expect you two do. I won a scholarship to the university. Zagreb University was founded in 1699, long before the United States, a fine old school, the top one in the country. As I'd always been interested in how things worked, especially radios, I decided to study electrical engineering. It was a new field back then and for that very reason a smart choice."

The old man cleared his throat and sipped the tea that had gone cold, like the house.

"When the war started, I was in my last year, only months from my degree. But my parents said I should get out of Croatia or I'd be drafted. 'War is terrible. Come back when it's over,' said Otac. 'Yes. Go to America,' Majka said bravely, trying to hide her sadness. 'I have a cousin there,' she said. 'First name Petar, last name Horvat. He lives in a town called Riverton in some place called Tennessee. You find him, he'll help,' she said, then burst into tears. I pray you never see *your* mother weep as mine did.

"I had little money when I landed in New York and my English wasn't good, though my passport was. A man in a uniform looked at it then hard at me, and said "Welcome." I was so nervous and such a greenhorn, I thought because he wore that uniform he could tell me how to get to Riverton. So, I asked. He made me repeat my question three times. My pronunciation wasn't perfect, the way it is now. He laughed and said, 'Oh, *Riverside*.' Then he pointed down the concourse toward a long desk with a crowd of people around it. It was the airport's tourist bureau. I picked up my cardboard old-world suitcase and took my place at the end of a line of middle-aged travelers with leather luggage, exasperated parents wrangling whining children, and excited people my own age in blue jeans with enormous backpacks.

"The longer I waited in that line the more confused I became and the more anxious. My head filled up with doubts and questions. Was it River*ton* or River*side* I was to go to? America is so much bigger than Croatia. The airport itself stretched out in every direction and seemed to me as vast as all of Zagreb. Would I be able to find the cousin who knew nothing of me? And even if I found my way to Petar Horvat, would he welcome me? He could have changed his name or moved elsewhere. In my nervousness I completely forgot about Tennessee. Your grandfather was a real mess that day, boys."

Stephen turned toward his brother and giggled. Will smiled at his brother and held a finger to his lips.

"When it was finally my turn, I asked the woman behind the counter how I could get to Riverton, then I said, no, to River*side*. She was impatient. 'Which is it?' she demanded. Remembering the man who checked my passport, I said it was Riverside. She made me say it again, slowly. '*Which* Riverside?' she asked. I was shaken. 'There's more than one?' Boys, do you know that *forty-six* states have a Riverside in them? It's the most common name for a town in the whole of America. As I'd forgotten all about Tennessee and had to say something, I asked what the biggest Riverside was. The woman tapped her busy colleague on the shoulder, whispered in his ear, got a reply, turned back to me and said, 'The one in California.' And so, I spent almost the last of my money on a bus ticket to Riverside, California. It took days and days. America, I thought, it's almost all highway. Everybody wants to be somewhere else."

By now, Stephen was squirming and Will couldn't resist the urge to move things along.

"When did you hear about the tornado, Grandpa?"

The old man frowned. "That was the year after I got my job."

"And it really destroyed all of Riverton, the one in Tennessee?"

"If I'd had better pronunciation and a clearer memory, I might have been there, among the dead."

"So Riverside was the *wrong* place but turned out to be the *right* one?"

"Yes. Bourns had set up its headquarters here. They hired me because business was taking off and they were desperate for electrical engineers, even one with poor English and no degree."

"And your boss's secretary was Grandma?" Stephen chimed in.

"And you invented two new transformers. Big sellers. And they promoted you."

"Then you and Grandma got married and had Mommy."

"And Mom met Dad and they had us."

"And here we all are!" shouted Stephen, jumping off the couch.

Hungry for breakfast, Will also got to his feet. "Just think. What if you'd remembered Riverton and Tennessee!"

Peeved that the boys pre-empted his story, the old refugee raised a finger spoke sternly.

"There's a lesson for you. In this world things happen in three ways."

"What are they?" asked Will, trying to sound interested as he yanked his exasperated brother back toward the couch.

"Some things happen by choice—like your mother. Some happen by necessity—like leaving Croatia. But most things happen by chance."

"Chance?"

"Yes. In fact, you could say that my career, my marrying Grandma, your mother getting born, her marrying your father, and the both of you all come from a mix-up. But nobody likes hearing that. They want their lives to be meaningful, the result of their choices. So they call chance fate." Here the old man pointed at the lightless tree. "Or, if they're religious, they call it God's plan. So, be humble."

"Yes, Grandpa."

"Be humble and hope to be lucky like me."

"Can we have breakfast *now*?" Stephen begged.

"Just one more thing—don't interrupt your elders."

Izels

Three weeks after Izel Mahmudov was awarded the Rheinach Prize for Medical Research, two FBI agents entered his laboratory and, making no effort to spare him humiliation before his colleagues, took him into custody.

"What have I done?" he asked the agents. "Where are you taking me?"

During the last years of the lengthy and brutal ethnic war in his country, Izel completed his medical studies in the relative safety of the capital. In his final year, news reached him that the village where he had grown up was attacked and his parents killed. He had no siblings and had never been close to his uncle, two aunts, or four cousins. He assumed they were either dead or scattered. Except for a few friends and his work, Izel found himself alone in the world. Like many young, educated people in his country, he was eager to get out.

Izel was lucky. He was granted a refugee visa thanks to the sponsorship of a senior researcher at Spingold-Walker Pharmaceuticals. This kind man had read a brilliant paper on which Izel's name appeared as co-principal investigator alongside that of a well-established researcher. The Spingold-Walker scientist rightly concluded that, though the lab and whatever funds supported it belonged to the senior investigator, the work itself was Mahumudov's. He contacted Izel through the university where he earned his degree. Izel begged for help in emigrating and Spingold-Walker took care of everything on condition that he come and work for them.

Izel Mahmudov gratefully accepted employment with S-W, found a studio apartment within walking distance of the laboratories, and applied for citizenship. The breakthrough that won Izel the Rheinach Prize was the first effective treatment for Hedwegh's Sarcoma, an invariably lethal form of cancer. Thanks to Izel's work, lives were extended and Spingold-Walker's stock price shot up.

The post-war government in Izel's homeland needed some time to compile its first list of war criminals. Investigations had to be conducted, witnesses interviewed, and, where they existed, records checked. The process was complicated by political compromises and bribes. Given the difficulties and the zeal of some of the investigators, errors were perhaps to be expected.

A prominent name on the list at last distributed to the world was that of Izel Mahmudev. When the war broke out, this man, a fanatic nationalist who had just completed a degree in ophthalmology, volunteered for the anti-government forces. During the years of conflict, he had charge of a prisoner-of-war camp, one notorious even amidst the general barbarity for its atrocities. In addition to murders and starvation Mahmudev presided over tortures, the most unspeakable of which he personally devised.

The inventory of wanted war criminals was turned over to the government's Rights Violators and War Crimes Center whose first task was to crosscheck it against a list of recent visa-holders and immigrants. The investigator assigned names from K through N immediately flagged Izel Mahmudov as a person whose visa should at once be revoked and deportation proceedings opened. He did take note of the fact that the name on between on the war criminals list was Izel Mahmud*ev* and Izel Mahmud*ov* on the visa list, but a Google search informed him the two spellings of patronymic surnames are interchangeable. There were no photographs of Mahmudev available, but the information that the criminal held a medical degree confirmed that he must be the pharmaceutical researcher Mahmudov.

Izel Mahumudov's company lawyer was skillful. He was able to keep the case dragging on for seven months, at the end of which Izel was deported.

Meanwhile, Izel Mahmudev adopted the name Istvan Markovic, preserving his old initials, and moved to a small town in a rural district far from the capital. Here he established a modest practice correcting the vision of peasants, policemen, and provincial dignitaries.

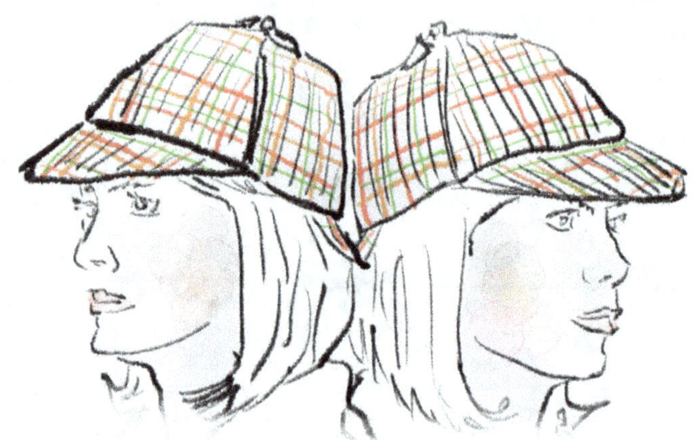

Yezhovshchina

The purges had swollen from liquidating Party members to reducing the general population, and the indefatigably compliant four-foot-eleven, forty-two-year-old Nikolai Ivanovich Yezhov had been put in charge of the People's Commissariat of Internal Affairs. Not long before his one-way trip to the Kommunarka shooting ground, Nikolai Bukharin had written, "In the whole of my—now, alas, already long life—I had to meet few people who, by their nature, were as repellent as Yezhov." And yet Yezhov knew how to charm. Only a few years before, Nadezhda Mandelstam, not yet a widow, described him as a "modest and rather agreeable person."

The General Secretary liked Yezhov for his dog-like fealty, his poverty of scruples and wealth of sadism, but perhaps most of all for his diminutive stature. Joseph Vissarionovich himself stood only five-foot-five. At Potsdam, Harry Truman, at five-eight, once referred to him as a "little squirt." Perhaps the day this remark of the President was reported to Stalin was the one the Cold War started.

On November 11, 1937, Nastya Mikhailovna Plokiyov decided to visit Comrade Yezhov. Her husband, Gerasim Fyodorovich, was chief deputy to Vyacheslav Molotov, not yet foreign minister, but Chairman of the Council of People's Commissars of the USSR. Nastya Mikhailovna, a tall, good-looking woman, fifteen years younger than her uxorious and overweight spouse, liked to dress fashionably. Her wardrobe, among the best in Moscow, included imported dresses and high-heeled shoes which she received as gifts from the Western diplomats she mixed with at receptions and with whom she occasionally and discreetly slept. Her opinion of Gerasim, whom she could barely stand but knew well how to deceive, was much like Bukharin's of Yezhov.

Nastya Mikhailovna wanted out of her marriage but, because of her husband's position, going to the courts was unthinkable. Seeking a divorce would, at a minimum, cost her status and protection. Still, the prospect of more years with Gerasim was intolerable. When she came across an article in *Pravda* extolling a twelve-year-old girl who had informed on her parents for listening to short-wave broadcasts, she formulated a bold plan. Telling him she was studying English, she asked one of her particular friends, a counselor at the British embassy, for some books. He gave her three in a Harrod's bag. He had wrapped them in thick brown paper tied up not with string but heavy rope. Nastya, who spoke Russian like the native she was, but knew no English words except "Yes, my dear" and only a few polite dinner-party phrases in French, was unable to read any of them.

On November 11, dressed elegantly but demurely, she put one of the books in her handbag and presented herself at the forbidding Lubyanka. Taking no notice of the swarm of armed guards, she walked straight to the reception desk, identified herself as the wife of Gerasim Plokiyov, and said that she wished to see the Chief on a matter of urgency, haughtily declaring that she would speak only with Comrade Yezhov. The two uniformed men behind the desk looked her up and down. The one she had addressed frowned; the other looked confused and picked up his phone. Evidently, messages passed from floor to floor, always upward, away from the dungeons below. Nastya was shown into a small room off the lobby. It was furnished with a thick Caucasian rug, a large potted plant (*Monstera deliciosa*), two matching armchairs, and a leather love seat. The guard who had conducted her to the room waited with her. Here she sat impatiently crossing and recrossing her long legs, at which the stoical guard pretended not to look. She clutched her bag to her chest. After half-an-hour, an official came in blowing his nose. He wore a badly tailored blue suit and looked a good deal like Gerasim.

"Comrade Yezhov has agreed to see you. Come with me."

The official wheezed a good deal and struggled to keep up with Nastya as they mounted the stairs to the top floor.

"Come," he gasped, and walked her to the door at the back of a wide room filled with men and women typing away. They all looked up furtively without stopping. "You're expected."

Yezhov's office was as much on a grand scale as he was not. The little man, nicknamed The Bloody Dwarf in whispers, had risen high on the corpses of people at whose murders he had connived. He sat behind a colossal desk, dwarfed by it.

The official announced her and Yezhov got briefly to his feet, though his head was no higher than it had been when he was seated. His face struck Nastya as rather handsome, though the smile with which he greeted her looked as if it might crack an underlying grimness. He waved the Gerasimesque official away.

He did not ask Nastya to sit. He couldn't have as there were no chairs other than his own.

"I'm told, Nastya Mikhailovna," he said in a high-pitched voice, "that you've asked to see me on a matter of urgency. I presume this means you have knowledge of some danger to the state." Then he posed the two questions he had asked many times before. "What is it? Whom does it concern?"

Nastya did not pretend to be reluctant to reply. She was as direct as Yezhov had been.

"It is about disloyalty, Comrade Yezhov, and it concerns my husband, Gerasim Fyodorovich Plokiyov."

"I believe your husband occupies a position of trust in the office of Comrade Molotov."

"Misplaced trust, Comrade."

"Yes?"

"My husband is in contact—unofficially, you understand—with a counselor at the British embassy whom I believe to be an intelligence agent."

"A most serious charge. Have you proof?" Yezhov looked at her sternly, but Nastya didn't flinch.

She opened her bag and handed the book to Yezhov. "He is receiving reading matter from the Englishman. It could be subversive literature or, as I suspect, the key to a code."

Yezhov raised his eyebrows. "A code?"

"A letter code. I've read about them."

Yezhov paged indifferently through the book.

"So, you think your husband should be arrested and questioned?"

"I do. Yes."

Yezhov smiled at Nastya. It was not a warm smile.

He held up the book. "Do you know what this is?"

"I have no English," said Nastya proudly, as if her ignorance was a proof of her patriotism.

"This is a collection of stories by Sir Arthur Conan Doyle, Sherlock Holmes stories. This book was banned in 1929; however, the First Secretary is personally an admirer of Doyle. He has even made copies of this book available to a select group of officials, people like me. For training the mind, he said."

Nastya did not know what to say.

"As it happens," said Yezhov coldly, "we have a file on your husband."

Nastya evinced no surprise. No one in Russia would.

"But," said the Chief of the NKVD, "we have a far thicker one on you."

Yezhov pushed a button. Two guards, both over six feet tall, entered at once. Each took one of Nastya's shapely arms and escorted her down all six floors to the cellars.

The Memory Unit

Saint Jeanne's Home sits on a large, well-maintained campus in rural Allegheny County. The grounds feature copper beeches, blue spruces, box hedges, rhododendrons, spirea and the kind of lawn that summons up English country estates. There is a gold cross on the peak of the portico. Saint Jeanne's is a first-class care facility and not cheap. The charge is $5000 a month for what is called, without irony, assisted living. The price for those housed in the special unit named for Saint Dymphna, patron of the demented, is nearly twice as much. The memory unit has eighteen individual rooms each with its own bathroom ensuite with elevated commodes and handrails everywhere. Nine rooms are on the east side, nine on the west. In between there is a kitchen area for snacks, tables and chairs for meals, and a vast flat-screen TV confronting eighteen recliners. To enter or leave the unit requires a code. Almost all the residents are women and the same goes for the staff who were all born in hot countries far from Allegheny County.

Eighty-three-year-old George Demetrios was one of two men in the memory unit. He had been a successful restaurateur in Pittsburgh, married with two children and five grandchildren. A gregarious man, he relished chatting with his customers, was liked by the newer staff and adored by the veterans. When his memory went, his wife Yvonne took over the business and moved George to Saint Jeanne's over her husband's objections. To the reservations of their children, she replied, "You don't have to live with him while trying to run three restaurants." Yvonne visited, on average, every three weeks and spent most of the hour she was there upbraiding the staff and interrogating the management. At first, George did sometimes recognize her, but twice he guessed she was his mother and three times thought she was his deceased sister. In time, he didn't recognize her at all. But his genial sociability was proof against his dementia, and he was always glad to see everybody, including Yvonne. Holding out his hand, as he did to all visitors, he would cordially, "Hello! So glad you to see you. I'm George. You look like you're having a lovely day. What's your name?" He asked all visitors about the weather and usually told them a joke, most often the one about a Greek immigrant who had no

English. His cousin got him a construction job but forgot to teach him how to order lunch at the local diner. So, the cousin made him repeat the phrase "ham sandwich" until his accent was penetrable. When, after a week of eating nothing but ham sandwiches, the kindly waitress asked, "Would you like some apple pie and coffee with that?" the panicked immigrant shouted, "Ham sandwich!"

George was a favorite with all the women in the unit, including the staff. Rarity confers value. The only other man in the unit, though much younger, seldom came out of his room. The poor fellow, a victim of early onset Alzheimer's, had no visitors and hardly said a word to anyone.

Marsha Kelleher's decline began when the dress shop she managed for thirty-two years closed and she couldn't find another job. Her husband's death three years later moved things into high gear. Her daughter sold the big house and moved Marsha in with her after putting in a third bathroom. Marsha grew morose, cried often, and lost touch with her friends. She was unsteady on her feet, far beyond forgetful, and occasionally incontinent. Around-the-clock home aides didn't aid enough. Her daughter, her son-in-law, and teenage grandson all grew desperate. Finally, everybody, including Marsha, agreed the money from the house would go for Saint Jeanne's.

Marsha was initially disoriented and stayed close to her room or in it. But years of helping women clothe and decorate themselves had formed habits. She soon engaged with the other women in the unit, cheerfully advising them on their appearance, treating them alternately as customers and children. George liked this about Marsha and the look of her, too. He introduced himself to her every morning for four days, sat with her at meals, and showed her pictures of youngsters, though he couldn't recall their names or whether they were his children or grandchildren. He never mentioned Yvonne or being married because he couldn't remember either. For some reason, he called Marsha Monica, and, surprisingly, she accepted the new name. Soon she wouldn't answer to any other. Marsha/Monica liked George who was tall and funny and made her feel special. The staff were benignly amused to see how the two were with each other. "Like a couple of teenagers," one commented. "So cute," another cooed. Marsha's daughter was delighted to see her mother happy again and, like everybody else, she liked George.

George and Monica spent most days together, except for naps and medical checkups. Neither had any interest in the stupefying daytime television that mesmerized the others. The nature of their relationship or even identities was not fixed for them. Monica told her daughter that George was her boyfriend then that they were engaged, holding up her hand with the two diamond rings she always wore. Sometimes she said they were married. As for George, he was simply smitten, perhaps holding a torch for some long-ago Monica. His brief bouts of withdrawal and depression ceased; he was even more cheerful than before. He never mentioned having a wife; Monica never referred to having had a husband. She called her daughter "Mom."

They were two rays of sunshine in the dull dusk of the demented. Rather surprisingly, their happiness was not a cause of envy but rather a font of universal satisfaction. The other women accepted them as a married couple. The two of them, though wrapped up in each other, made time for everybody else. Monica went on discussing make-up, blazers, lingerie, and jewelry with the old ladies. George told them amusing stories about his childhood and, in an inconsequential but flattering way, flirted with them. He stopped whispering requests to the staff for a big bottle of sleeping pills and/or a shotgun. Monica no longer whined, "I want to go home." She no longer remembered the home.

Then, one day, the two napped together in George's room. The staff informed the unit manager who told them this was forbidden, but the next night George slipped into Monica's room and stayed. The sympathetic staff were perplexed, but not for long. On George's wife's next visit, one of them, believing it her Catholic duty, told George's wife about Marsha/Monica, including the unauthorized sleeping.

Yvonne Demetrios took her rage straight to the top, the executive director, an ex-nun who understood her primary concern to be the satisfaction of those who paid and only secondarily that of the inmates.

"I'm not paying seventy grand a year to subsidize my husband's adultery. This place has got crucifixes plastered all over it. It's named for a *saint*, for Christ's sake. Fix this or I'm shipping him out. Got it?"

Strict orders were issued. Marsha was moved from the east to the west side. George was prevented from sitting with her during meals. Staff were instructed to keep them apart by means of distraction, feeding them at different times, changing the nap schedule, and, when these measures failed, gentle but straightforward physical interference.

Marsha/Monica grew depressed. She wept when her daughter visited but also when she didn't. As for George, his mood changed. One afternoon, he tied his sheets together and tried to hang himself from the showerhead which broke, causing a minor flood. When he saw Marsha, he wanted to reach out but couldn't recall her name. He no longer recognized Yvonne as either his wife or his sister. When she visited, he introduced himself and told her about the immigrant and the ham sandwich.

Marsha's daughter made an appointment with the executive director.

"Aren't you supposed to make these poor people as happy as possible? Isn't that your *job*?" Though she was no longer a nun, the director told Marsha the story of Saint Dymphna, beheaded at fifteen by her senile father because she refused to marry him.

"There *are* rules, my dear," she said frostily.

Marsha died in her sleep. Her cheeks were still wet in the morning. Three days later, George had a heart attack over dinner, the massive kind. His chair tipped over and he fell to the floor. The staff was unable to revive him before the ambulance arrived.

Politics

Jennifer and John Jefferson had two sons, Jared, ten, and James, eight. James, who preferred Jim, was skilled at provoking his brother who never called him Jim. He called him "Jar-Head" and "Jorrid," and did things like putting wet washcloths in his bed and hiding vital Lego pieces. To retaliate, Jared would leave post-it notes for his brother with questions like "How long did the Hundred Years War last?" and "In what state would you find Indiana University?" so he could correct him. "Actually, it was a hundred and sixteen years." "It's in Pennsylvania. Look it up." He called his little brother "Jimbecile" and "Cement-Head." Jared always got perfect grades; James didn't. James was good at every kind of sport; Jared wasn't.

Jennifer's method of dealing with her boys was simple. The more worked-up they got, the calmer she became; the louder their voices, the softer she made hers. This worked well because both boys adored her; and, though this was itself at the root of their abrasive rivalry, neither wanted Jennifer to be mad at him, just at his brother.

One day, Jennifer baked a chocolate sheet cake. It was on the kitchen counter when the boys got home from school. They burst through the door arguing about Ms. Pitt who had been Jared's teacher two years before and was now James'. Jared thought she was wonderful; James hated her because of how often she compared him to his brainy brother. "Teacher's pet!" he shouted with contempt. "Jimbecile!" Jared retorted smugly.

"Quiet down, you two," said Jennifer then gave each a long and soothing hug.

The boys spotted the cake.

"Can *I* have some?" both said. Neither said, "Can *we* have a piece?"

"It's for dessert."

"Aw, Mom," whined James.

"Please?" begged James. "I'm famished."

The boys looked at her pleadingly with extravagantly watering mouths. "I have to run to the dry cleaners," said Jennifer, realizing that this wasn't an answer. "Well, all right. You can each take a small piece off the side." She laid a knife on the counter. "Be *very* careful with this."

"I will," said Jared.

"Me, too," Jim echoed.

"*Bon voyage, Maman*," said Jared, who was teaching himself French.

Jared insisted on taking the knife first on grounds of seniority. He cut a small slice off the left side of the cake and laid the knife down on the counter.

"Just a *small* piece, and be very careful with the knife," he warned his brother.

"*Be careful with the knife,*" James said in the falsetto he used to mock his bossy brother.

The cake was delicious, moist, chocolaty inside and on top.

James looked hard at the cake, the knife, and his brother.

"She didn't actually say *one* piece."

Jared, surprised by his brother's astuteness, considered his point. "Or one *time*."

"Right!"

So, each cut another slice, one from the left, the other from the right, bigger ones this time.

Jared got the milk from the refrigerator. James went to the cupboard and took out two glasses.

They cut more slices, from each side. The middle got narrower, thinner, tinier, until scarcely even a sliver was left.

Politics

The New Dentist

Five years ago, Fred Nielsen drove his Honda into town and bought Doc Fitz's practice from his widow Sylvia. The Doc had been gone just over a week. Nielsen took over the lease on the office, purchased all the equipment along with what the brokers call Goodwill, which pretty much means that Nielsen paid Sylvia something extra for keeping all Doc's patients. That was generous rather than necessary. We're a one-dentist town; it's thirty-six miles one-way to the next nearest. Gertie Hartsel, Fitz's long-time hygienist, might have been part of the deal, too. The change was seamless; people were relieved.

Nielsen was a good dentist, better than Doc Fitz. But, once people got over seeing him as a gift horse, they got curious to check out his mouth; some were suspicious. For one thing, we're a three-church town and he didn't join any of them. To be un-churched is nearly to be half a citizen, cut off from the town's social life. Then there was the timing; a new dentist showing up so shortly after the old one's death didn't feel like luck. Most of all, though, there was Nielsen himself. He was around forty, good-looking, with an Ivy League degree. He drove into town in a Honda Accord with two suitcases, no wife and no kids, registered at the Billingson's B and B, and the next day made straight for Sylvia Fitzpatrick's house and wrapped up their deal just after lunch. Nielsen rented the Folsoms' two-bedroom ranch house on the edge of town, right before the wheat fields begin. When her mother brought Debbie Holst in for a filling the next week, Debbie told Nielsen that their mutt had a litter and he bought one of puppies. People around here think it's a compliment to say of somebody that they keep to themselves, but we don't really like it. This is the sort of a town where everybody knows everybody else's business; for most of us, the new dentist kept too much to himself. We didn't know his religion, his people; we didn't even know why he was here. He had arrived like any godsend—out of the blue and unexplained. We knew the new dentist's profession but we didn't know his business.

My own business is running the town's pharmacy and my vocation is fly-fishing and I'm better at the latter than the former. I'd see Fred Nielsen regularly when he came in to pick up dental supplies, but also things for himself, toothpaste, floss, razor blades, after-shave, band aids, aspirin and such. I'd try to get him talking, figuring he might be more forthcoming with a fellow health professional, but he wasn't. He was polite enough. He smiled and always had a pleasant greeting, a courteous farewell; but he seemed shut in, closed down. It made me sad to look at him, sad the way the women who tried to fix him up felt, only less angry. I guess it was more my own sadness than his that gave me the idea of getting him up to Verdigre Creek.

He admitted he'd done a little fishing back east when he was a kid, dropping a line with a worm on the end of it. Once, he said, the uncle of a friend took a bunch of boys out onto the ocean when the bluefish were running. He hadn't liked it. He said he'd gotten sick, didn't catch anything, and didn't care for the beer-swilling and boastful uncle either.

I explained that fly-fishing was to what he'd done as skilled oral surgery was to yanking molars with a pair of pliers, as Maker's Mark was to Bud Light, as a Zen master was to a televangelist. I observed that no one got seasick fishing in a trout stream and that I had an extra pair of waders and a good Orvis pole and about fifty dry flies but that any day on the Verdigre was a good one, whether you caught anything or not. He didn't jump at my invitation but I didn't let it drop and eventually I suppose he was bored enough to give in.

I got him to come to dinner on a Tuesday. While Doris set the table and after I got us both a beer, I took him out back and showed him how to throw a line, what to do with his wrist, how to aim and let the fly settle. He caught on quickly, which pleased me, and then had three helpings of my wife's pot roast, which delighted her. A pot roast is a thing a single man won't make for himself, Doris later explained smugly. I made him take the Orvis home so he could practice and told him to be ready to be picked up at four-thirty Saturday morning.

It was a fine spring morning, about perfect. The air was brisk and bright, the water cold from melting snow.

We each caught two fish, which I told him was good. I helped him release his catch, extracting the fly carefully, for which he was grateful. "Busman's holiday," I joked. "I guess you spend enough time in mouths."

"I read somewhere that trout are smart," he said.

"They are."

I asked him impertinent questions over the lunch Doris had packed for us. "So, how'd you come to pick Nebraska?" "Planning any trips? "Things go south back east?" He parried my thrusts easily so my leading questions led nowhere.

It was on the drive back that I got the story—his story, at least *a* story. I suppose he might have made the tale up to stop me from fishing for one, but I think he told me the truth because I was watching the road rather than his face. It's not impossible that he told me a ridiculous whopper he was sure I'd believe, and then, through me, so would the whole town. Well, if the story he told me had been more plausible and more to his credit, I might believe that. But, as it's neither, I'm ninety percent sure what he told me is the truth if, that is, the truth is what he himself believes.

... I had a good practice, a good life. Cecilia and I met as undergrads at NYU and married when I finished dental school at Penn. We found this house we loved in Harrison, Westchester County, about twenty miles north of Manhattan. It was more than we could afford. I was just getting started and we really needed two salaries. Cecilia agreed with me that we should put off having kids. Anyway, she liked her job. She managed fund-raising for a non-profit that supported indigent new mothers. It meant a lot of work at home and commuting twice a week into the city but she liked it and, in a sense, she was looking after a lot of children.

One of the old NYU gang was my best friend, Charlie Steinberg. After floundering for a couple years, he went into the family business in investment banking, stockbroking. Charlie had a big place nearby in Rye and was married to a wonderful woman, Julia. They'd met in Italy when Charlie hadn't yet settled down, a couple of tourists who hit it off in a trattoria. They had two little girls. We socialized with them some—dinners, a couple of July fourth cookouts, a party next to Charlie's pool. We even took a two-week vacation together on Cape Cod, all six of us. Cecilia had the best time; she really bloomed, playing with the girls, chatting with Julia, joking around with Charlie.

Then Julia got sick. It was the kind of cancer that gallops. She was gone in three months. Charlie was devastated, depressed, helpless. Cecilia threw herself into helping. She took him food. She drove the girls places. She cleaned the house, made the beds, stocked the groceries. Whenever she didn't have to go to the city she was in Rye. She even stayed overnight several times. The girls had grown attached, she said; she couldn't let them down. They'd get better soon, but now they were needy.

How did I feel? First sympathetic, then neglected and ashamed, then resentful, envious, and finally jealous—real green-eyed monster jealous. I was sure Cecilia was screwing Charlie and vice versa. But I didn't confront either of them. It was probably cowardice but at the time I told myself I wouldn't believe any denials and a pair of confessions would make everything even worse.

So, I decided to balance the scales. My new hygienist Libby had been looking at me with big eyes since I hired her. She rubbed up against me. She worried that I wasn't eating healthy. She was pretty and willing, and she was twenty-four.

One afternoon at the Ramada, I got carried away and told Libby about Charlie and Cecilia. She could hardly be indignant so she tried to sound sympathetic, but I could see she was exultant. From that day on, Libby was sure I was going to divorce Cecilia and marry her. She just wanted to know when.

And I might have done it, too. But one night I came home to find Cecilia bursting, dying to tell me the good news. The news was that Charlie was engaged. It was one of those Facebook things: high school couple dates, dances, go off into their lives until one's divorced and the other's widowed and they reconnect more than just virtually. Kismet. A second act. Cecilia was over the moon with vicarious delight.

I got it all wrong. I had *them* all wrong but mostly *I* was wrong. Libby was pressing me to meet her parents and brothers and to see a lawyer. Cecilia said it was time we had a child but I could hardly look at her. I couldn't bring myself to visit Charlie either. I was shocked, embarrassed, stymied. I was in a jail I'd built for myself. The foundation was false, but the cell was real. The misunderstanding was too irreparable, too revealing, too stupid. I couldn't face it.

So, I took off. Just lit out. I kept a few thousand and put everything else in our joint account, took my name off it, and also the deed to the house. I signed over my IRA and left with some clothes and my diplomas.

Why your town? Because I knew Doc Fitz. We met at one of those vacations masquerading as professional conferences. This one was on implants, the latest thing, screws in bones. It was in Miami, sun and fun. Doc Fitz and I hit it off and so did the wives. Cecilia said it was like being adopted.

I was so sad when I sent my Christmas card and Sylvia wrote back that Fitz had just died.

Small town. No dentist. I figured it was worth a shot. I phoned Sylvia and made her an offer the day before I left.

For months I was scared, terrified that Cecilia or Libby—or, in my worst nightmares both of them—would hire detectives and track me down. I didn't want that. I couldn't face them. I can't even face *you*. What did I want? I wanted to kill whatever the instinct is for intimacy.

Nielsen walks his dog to his office every morning. Kids love the big gentle mutt. The new dentist is good with children. These days people call him Doc Nielsen; he isn't so new anymore.

I've never asked about what he told me, not even when I take him for an outing to flog a trout stream. If there really was a Cecilia, a Libby, a Charlie with two little girls and a second wife, then, so far as I know, they haven't come after him.

We all get things wrong, take the wrong turn, hold tight to a misjudgment. The trouble comes when we persist in the wrongness, if we cleave to a fixed idea. People too certain of their facts are like those too sure of their own virtue. They're the ones who steam right into the iceberg, who drive straight off the cliff.

Kims and Parks

Back in middle school I had a rascally friend. Lee Tae was a troublemaker. One afternoon he and I took a stroll down Hongdae Shopping Street. I walked right by the outdoor display racks, but Tae stopped and fingered the jeans, jackets, and shirts like a connoisseur. We hadn't gone to Hongdae to buy but to see what was cool. We walked from one store to another, passing lots of small shops named for their owners. Tae started to complain about how poor Korea is in family names.

"I keep meeting people named Lee and I don't know if we're related or not. What if I fell for a girl named Lee who was my cousin and we got married and had children born without ears or chins?" He got quite worked up. "It's absurd. Something ought to be done. We need more names!"

I calmly granted that, while there might be some, I personally had never heard of anybody having children born without chins and ears.

"That so?" scoffed Tae with the wicked gleam in his eye. I had seen that gleam before, whenever he was about to pull some stunt. He had the same look when, during recess, he maneuvered Choi Yunghee over the ventilation grate so it blew her skirt all the way up to her waist. She burst into tears and ran off. His round face wore the same expression on the morning that he stuffed a garden snake into the drawer of our teacher's desk.

We came to the corner just beyond the big Playground store.

"Watch this," said Tae. He halted, cupped his hands around his mouth, and shouted down one way, "Hey, Mr. Kim!" Then turned around and screeched, "Hey, Mrs. Lee!"

Scores of people stopped and stared our way. Others turned around, craning their necks to look for whoever had called them.

Tae crossed his arms. "See?" he said with a smirk and a complacent shrug.

It is true that we have few family names; and if every name is a story, then we share our stories with millions. Nevertheless, there are plenty of personal names by which we distinguish ourselves, at least in part.

Misunderstandings are bound to arise in our capital with its population of ten million. A big city is like one of those epic novels that start off with a list of characters with all their family trees that runs for pages. This is presumably to help readers keep everything straight, but it seldom works. No more can the life of a city be made smooth and predictable by laying out its streets in a grid and publishing a comprehensive telephone directory. The relationships among a city's inhabitants will never be as rational as the directory or the street map. No matter how sharp the corners, how accurate the listings, how legible the signs, there will still be surprises, muddles, accidents.

During my last year at Seoul National, I dated Park Ara, an attractive math major with good manners, a fine figure, and an affectionate nature. Ara had many virtues; in fact, looking back, her only real fault was an excessive devotion to her female friends. She was forever texting with them, inserting herself into their lives, updating them about herself and each other, broadcasting gossip. Ara felt a compulsion to know her friends' plans, their feelings, how they were getting on with their families and, above all, their love lives. One of these friends was Kim Chaelin, a third-year student from the south majoring in business. She might have imagined a brief career, but it would be followed by a future as a wife and mother. Ara said Chaelin knew whom she would marry and whose children she would bear because she had a longtime boyfriend. When this boyfriend suddenly broke things off, Chaelin was devastated. She dyed her hair green then purple, neglected her studies, even her hygiene. She lost weight and never laughed or smiled. In a voice thick with empathetic sorrow, Ara told me Chaelin spent hours alone in her room listening to the saddest songs of the time like Sook's "Summer Scent Serenade" and "No Matter How Many Times We Part" by Yoon Gun. That year there were five suicides at the University.

Ara was determined to do something. She begged me to fix one of my unattached friends up with Chaelin. "If losing her boyfriend has nearly destroyed her," she said, "isn't the cure obvious? Think of somebody."

I thought of Kim Hoon, a music major with whom I had played badminton a couple of times. I didn't know him well, but I considered him a good sort, courteous, a hard-working and ambitious student. He twice turned down my invitations for a game because he spent most of his free time playing the pianos in the University's practice rooms. I hesitated. Chaelin was evidently the emotional type; but Hoon, from what I'd observed, was either short on feelings or held on to them the way a sober poker player hides his cards. But then I considered the principle from physics that opposites attract. It might work out, I rationalized. My chief consideration was to stop my girlfriend whining about her friend and pestering me.

Anticipating resistance, I didn't text or phone Hoon. I tracked him down in the practice rooms and broached the matter face to face. He did need persuading. I warned him sententiously that too much practicing was as bad as too little and that his youth would be over before he knew it. I said that people were concerned about his isolating himself, being all work and no play. I told him that Chaelin was pretty and clever but didn't mention her depression.

Meanwhile, Ara asked her friend if she would be open to seeing somebody and that she had somebody in mind. Chaelin put up some resistance that Ara described as "half-hearted," but Ara argued that a blind date was better than dying her hair pink. Ara said that when Chaelin gave in she even smiled a little.

Thrilled and energized to be arranging the lives of others, Ara insisted I instruct Hoon that he should meet Chaelin at the most romantic spot in the city. I asked what that was.

"Silly, man," she said touching my nose. "The pavilion in Namsan Mountain Park."

"The Palgokjeong Pavilion? The octagonal one?"

She nodded. "From up there, the whole city's spread out like a picnic blanket." Then she rattled off the names of three restaurants to which she would approve of my friend taking hers.

The Palgokjeong Pavilion embodies some of the recent history of our country. It was originally built in 1959 to honor the dishonorable Rhee Syngman. A year later, the April 19 Movement forced Rhee out and demolished his pavilion. Eight years after that, it was rebuilt and renamed. Ever since, it has been a favorite spot with locals and tourists, also the site of the New Year's Sunrise Festival.

Ara was, of course, anxious that the date should go well for her friend. She twice mentioned the five student suicides. She would have liked to spy on Chaelin and Hoon, to watch everything. She even asked if we could join them, make it a double date. I explained why this was a bad idea and dissuaded her by saying that Hoon was so shy he would clam up if we horned in.

The couple was to meet on the steps of the pavilion at five-thirty on a Saturday afternoon. Ara worried about the weather. "What if it's pouring rain, or there's fog?" But as it turned out, the sky was clear that day, the air not too humid. Ara rejoiced that the couple would see the sun setting picturesquely just as the city fired up its neon signs. She insisted that we meet at the same time and spend the evening together. We met at five-thirty and it was all I could do to keep her from texting Chaelin minutes later. Then she said we should go to the restaurant Hoon had chosen. "We could sit somewhere where they can't see us." Instead of pointing out that this was another bad idea, I told Ara I didn't know which place Hoon had picked or if it was one of the three she prescribed. She pouted. We went for a walk then ate at a local restaurant, praised for its kimchi soup. Ara was on edge the whole time, checking her phone every few minutes. It was exasperating. At last, she got a text from Chaelin, squealed like a schoolgirl, and read it to me triumphantly, read it to me three times.

Hoon best medicine. Dinner a joy. Can't thank you enough. Talk tomorrow.

The following afternoon I got a call from Hoon thanking me as well. He said Chaelin was charming; that they had a lot more in common than I'd suggested, and that they would be seeing each other again that night. I told him I was glad to hear it. I was also surprised.

A week later, Ara phoned Chaelin and arranged the double date for which she had been itching. We were to meet at a new barbecue restaurant that had gotten top reviews online.

We met. Chaelin and Hoon glowed with an almost extravagant happiness.

There was only one problem. Hoon was not Hoon; that is, not *my* Hoon.

The vast city is like a novel of which Ara would have liked to be the author. Her favorite writer was Jane Austen. But, of course, our teeming city is not at all like an Austen novel. It is too complicated, its plots more like those of Charles Dickens, sprawling, inconclusive, prone to unpredictability, improvisation, loose ends, and improbable coincidences. Seoul has more than one Hoon, more than a single Chaelin.

It didn't take long to figure things out. There was another Park Chaelin, a second-year piano student at Dankook University School of Music. There was another Kim Hoon, a recent economics graduate from our own SNU. There was even another Ara—though this one's name was Yunghi—who also liked bringing couples together, who also deemed the octagonal pavilion at Namsam Park the ideal spot for a couple to meet at sunset. It wasn't hard to picture how it must have gone, two Chaelins and two Hoons on opposite sides of the pavilion, eyeing each other uncertainly, giving their names, shaking hands, watching the sun set, going off to eat.

All that happened almost ten years ago. Ara and I broke up right after we graduated. We married other people but are still occasionally in touch. That's how I know that "her" Chaelin wed the "wrong" Hoon and that they divorced three years later. According to Ara, this was because Chaelin wanted a child and Hoon didn't, because Hoon wanted to emigrate and Chaelin refused. I suspect it might also have been because they had become bored with one another and each had compiled a catalogue of imperfections and irritating habits they had discovered in one another—small protuberances but rubbed against every day.

"My" Hoon did not marry the other Chaelin, the one from Dankook University. They married other people yet formed a union that turned out to be durable. I still remember Hoon telling me the story. On their second date, he took the Dankook Chaelin to his favorite place, the Music School's basement practice rooms. They played for each other. Then they played together. Apparently, their first duet was Milhaud's exuberant *Scaramouche*.

These days, as you may know, the celebrated Park-Kim Piano Duo tours the world.

A Most Unpleasant Story

When Justine and Sheila came back from the ladies, Lauren was chatting with two good-looking men. Sheila had brought somebody from work, while Lauren and Justine were on their own—and on the hunt.

"That looks promising," Sheila said. "Good luck, especially with that blond one. He reminds me of one of those Commie posters. Or a Nazi one. Blonds with biceps."

Lauren chuckled. "One with a tractor, the other with a tank?"

"The other guy's not bad either. But I'm bespoke and I'm off. Have a great night. Call me tomorrow, any time after ten." Sheila peeled away and Justine made her way to the bar.

Lauren made the introductions, raising her voice to overcome the twenty-something crowd's racket.

She addressed the buff blond. "This is my friend, the one you asked about. Justine, this is Simon."

Simon smiled warmly, nodded.

"And I'm Vincent," said the dark-haired one, moving a bit closer to Lauren.

"Simon and Vincent," said Justine. "Got it."

"They come bearing gifts," said Lauren and pointed at two fresh Manhattans squatting primly on white cocktail napkins.

The flirting began without me, thought Justine.

"Manhattans in Manhattan," mused Vincent blithely.

"Two lovely Manhattanites in a magnificent Manhattan bar, drinking Maker's Mark Manhattans," Simon declaimed while looking Justine over like an antique dealer checking out a Queen Anne loveseat.

"Lauren was specific," said Vincent, moving even closer to Lauren. "About the Maker's Mark."

Lauren shrugged. "What can I say? I like what I like."

As Simon listed toward Justine, she caught a whiff of sandalwood. She was glad she'd gone for the tight cocktail dress.

Lauren and Vincent moved a little away and began trashing some movie they'd both seen.

Justine looked at Simon, deadpan. "Tell me a joke," she demanded.

It was one of her icebreakers, one of her tests.

Simon laughed and rubbed his chin. "A joke on demand? Well, okay, if you promise to tell me one, too."

"Deal."

"Okay. So, it's summertime. This high school kid is trying to make some extra money. He bikes to a fancy neighborhood, knocks on doors, asks if anybody wants their lawn mown, hedges trimmed, has any odd jobs. Rich guy sticks his head out of his air-conditioned mansion, looks the kid up and down, and says yeah. He wants his porch painted, painted orange, and offers a hundred bucks. The kid's thrilled. A hundred. The man tells him everything he needs is in the garage, that some friends are picking him up for a round of golf, and he'll be back in two hours. When he gets back, the kid's waiting, looking pleased with himself and asking for his money. The porch hasn't been touched. What's up? the man demands. The kid smiles proudly and says it's all done. In fact, he says, there was so much paint, he put on two coats. Oh, and by the way, your Porsche? It's actually a Maserati."

Though she didn't think much of it, Justine laughed. "I like jokes about misunderstandings," she said. "But tell me the truth. That's really one of those dumb blonde jokes, isn't it?"

Simon blushed. "Busted," he said and pretended to pout fetchingly. "Okay, your turn."

Justine remembered a joke from a surprisingly lively linguistics elective she took her junior year. She'd had a brief crush on the young professor.

"Okay. A road down south. Macho guy's tooling along in his pickup and comes to the bottom of this steep hill. A woman in a convertible comes over the hill, slows and yells "Pig!" The guy's enraged. He tosses her the bird and yells, "Bitch!" Then he floors it, roars up over the hill, and crashes into a huge sow in the middle of the road. Messes up his face, breaks two ribs, totals his truck."

Simon, laughing companionably, leaned in still closer. "Totaled the sow too, I'll bet."

Lauren and Vincent came back to take their leave. Lauren grinned like it was her sixteenth birthday. Vincent nodded at Simon.

Justine gave Lauren a quick farewell hug and turned back to Simon, "Favorite books?"

Simon thought for a moment then said he favored Russian novels with double names. "You know, *War and Peace, Crime and Punishment, Fathers and Sons, Life and Fate*. The kind that are so long you feel like you're living a sort of alternate life."

"How about *The Master and Margarita*?"

"A gem," he said. "One of your favorites?"

"Uh-huh."

"Okay. My turn now. Favorite movie stars?"

"Cary Grant, Marlon Brando, Bill Nighy."

"No women?"

"Katherine Hepburn, Jeanne Moreau, Meryl Streep."

"Two dead, and one still alive, like with the actors," Simon observed, and sipped his Manhattan.

"Your Russian novels are even older than my actors. Old-fashioned, aren't we?"

"A pair of fuddy-duddies, I guess."

The next hour of banter went well, excitingly, with another round of Manhattans.

Justine, buzzed, invited Simon back to her apartment in SoHo, a studio which, with her exiguous salary from a tiny but adventurous publishing house, she could afford only with a parental subsidy.

They slept late on Saturday. Justine woke first, after nine. She made coffee, bacon, eggs, and a toasted everything bagel for Simon. She had her usual yogurt and blueberries.

"Mmm," said Simon from the bed. "I love the smell of bacon in the morning."

"Even turkey bacon?"

"Yum. Almost healthy."

They giggled together, touched each other, made love, showered, then Simon left, and Justine walked on air the rest of the morning.

At noon, she phoned Lauren. Things had not gone well with Vincent.

"Turns out he's a bit of a pig," she said. "You and Simon?"

"Wonderful, actually."

"Spill."

Justine Kuszalt was raised Catholic Lite. There were masses, but not masses of masses. She attended public school and went to CCD classes. She picked up that sex was wrong and dangerous unless you were married. In high school, she capably repelled the urgency of her dates, endured their pleas and occasional insults. She was pretty and knew that was what mattered.

Justine's grades were good enough for the Ivies or the Seven Sisters, but she enrolled in the state university, like her older sister Jemma. The price was still steep for her family; a work-study job in the bursar's office helped.

In her sophomore year, she pledged a sorority, the one with the most popular coeds. She was shocked by the way the girls talked, what they talked about, by their drinking and most of all by their sexual competition. Justine's father, an Air Force veteran and a licensed electrician, was a WWII buff. She'd watched a lot of movies and documentaries with him. Though she was grossed out by the sisters who taped used condoms to their doors on Sunday mornings, it made her think of victorious fighter pilots who painted rising suns and swastikas on their Hellcats and Mustangs.

Justine got drunk on beer at her first frat party. She lost her virginity at the second and cried about it to her roommate, who told the sisters. The sorority threw her a party with a cake, rum punch, and streamers. She got a diaphragm, watched her drinking, and was selective. She didn't join the competition, but she did keep track of it. She enjoyed sex. It was fun, recreational, stress-reducing. She liked experimenting, changing partners without any strings attached.

Simon Legnari and his identical twin Spencer were from infancy extraordinarily, even bafflingly close—siblings sans rivalry. They never fought, hardly ever disagreed. When they were little, their parents dressed them the same and thought it amusing when one pretended to be the other. Fooling their parents was fun and reinforced. When they started school, they fooled their classmates and later their teachers, which was even better. Nobody could tell them apart. They moved into the big world but retained a little city of their own with a population of two. They had private jokes, codes, references, their own slang. They were sporty, liked working out together. They were good doubles players and won a championship. They enjoyed rowing together and for a time tried synchronized diving. The twins shared everything from their socks to their sweatshirts, their fondness for Monty Python and Martha Grimes and distaste for eggplant and German films. "The Tinder Box" was the favorite fairy tale of both, roast beef their favorite meal. They both wore boot-cut jeans, white Reeboks, Bass Weejuns, and black blazers. They preferred the same novels and porn stars—all Russian.

It was in high school that they started sharing girlfriends. This wasn't to bring them closer together; nothing could. It was more the other way around; they were so close in all things, why not this as well? It made their intimacy more intimate and gave them a lot to talk about. They relished comparing their experiences with girls, loved it far more than the girls. There was even teamwork of a sort. If Simon got to first base, Spencer would try to steal second. If Spencer made it to third, Simon would try for home. They favored the girls with bad reputations and only one of them ever figured it out. That was Marybeth Nowak who thought it was better than fine. She had her own game, guessing which was which, and what she did with one she would try to outdo with the other.

In their senior year, Simon and Spencer decided to go to NYU. Neither wanted to leave the city, the Yankees, Knicks, or Giants; neither was willing to live too far from Wall Street, the capital of the world and the setting for their future. In addition, they had heard that NYU had a lot of gay undergrads and figured, if it were true, there would be less competition in harvesting coeds, especially if they were feeling cheated, deprived, horny.

It was Simon who spent Friday night with Justine but Spencer who phoned Sunday morning. The weather was fine, and Justine thought it would be nice to have a picnic in Hudson River Park. She suggested they meet at Pier 25, by the minigolf. Spencer said he'd bring a blanket, Prosecco, and pick up a basket from Zabars. Simon had shown his brother plenty of jpgs, so he recognized Justine just as quickly as she did him.

It was dusk, the blue hour, as they meandered past the ferry slip and toward the Battery, when Justine suddenly pulled Spencer close, kissed him, and said she loved him—though, of course, she thought Spencer was Simon.

The affair continued for three weeks, nearly a record for the twins.

Then, one night, Spencer asked Simon, "Are you in love with Justine?"

"In love? Nope. You?"

"Not even a little bit. Anyway, you're the one she says she's in love with."

"Just checking."

"But the sex is really wonderful."

"Sure has been."

"I've been thinking things have, you know, run their course with Justine."

"Well yeah, maybe. We could definitely use more time with Vanessa."

"And Sumi. Don't forget Sumi!"

Simon didn't call for two days then said he'd be out of town on business for the weekend. Justine said she'd miss him. Her period was late, but she didn't want to say anything. She bought a test, awaited the result with dread. The short wait was long. Two pink lines. She gasped, felt scared and, for ten minutes was a little hysterical.

Then she felt something else, a positive feeling she couldn't name. She took deep breaths and made a cup of herbal tea to calm down before phoning Simon. She got his voice mail. "It's me. Call me. It's important." When he didn't call back, she kept trying, pleading that it was urgent. Finally, at around dinner time, he picked up.

"Sorry," he fibbed. "Had my phone turned off. Been in meetings all day. Clients. Investors. What's up?"

"I'm pregnant, that's what."

Simon felt his stomach tumble down to his crotch.

"Shit," he said in a strangled voice. "Jesus Christ. Bad news."

"Well, yes."

"But how?"

"You know how. Remember that time?"

"No, I don't. But, well, it's abortion time now."

"What?"

"What else?"

Justine was stunned, felt the panic rising. Her Catholic upbringing hadn't prevented premarital sex, lots of it; but it had inscribed a red line bolder than those two pink ones.

"I'm going to have the baby," she said resolutely and more icily than she meant to. "I mean, we are."

Simon had been thinking fast. "*We*? How do I even know it's mine?"

Justine gasped and started to weep, then she howled her fury into the phone.

Simon hung up.

Spencer's view of the matter was the same as Simon's. Fatherhood just wasn't on the agenda, marriage not on the menu.

"Anyway, I'm tired of Justine. She was always too clingy."

"And needy."

"And she snores, sometimes."

"Damn. Birth and death," Spencer mused philosophically. "They can both really screw up your plans."

Simon chuckled, albeit nervously.

They talked it through that night and decided not to take any calls from Justine, not to reply to her texts.

"We ghost her."

Justine kept phoning Simon, sent texts, then a long letter. When she came to their apartment, they didn't buzz her in. They hid.

A thick envelope arrived addressed to Mr. Simon Lagnari. It was from a lawyer. Justine was suing. They read the attorney's letter and the legal document that came with it over and over.

Spencer and Simon wanted inconsequential lives, lives without consequences, comic lives. Fatherhood, marriage, they were consequences. They were for later, much later. A paternity suit wasn't funny and a radioactive boulder even less.

They stewed in its shadow.

"Should we get a lawyer?"

"I don't know. Maybe. There's Jeremy, but he only graduated two years ago. And Brett, but I don't trust him."

"Dad? He's got two lawyers."

"No. We don't want Dad involved," said Spencer firmly. Then he broke into a sly smile.

"Bro, you've got an idea."

"I do indeed."

Since their teens, the brothers had collected news stories and magazine articles about identical twins. There was one about twins whose umbilical cords got tangled but who, according to the doctors, avoided suffocating in the womb by hugging each other. Another was about identical twins who married identical twins, then divorced within a week of each other. There was the story of twins adopted as newborns by different families and reunited at forty to discover that both had become pediatricians, suffered from tension headaches, bit their nails, smoked Salems, drove Volkswagen Jettas, and took their vacations in Coral Gables, Florida.

Spencer fetched the file and extracted two yellowed newspaper articles held together with a rusty staple.

"Remember?"

"Remember what?"

"The German thieves?"

"Ah, sure! One of my favorites."

"Mine, too. Especially now."

In the early hours of Sunday, January 25, 2009, three persons made their way to the roof of the Kaufhaus des Westens, Berlin's premier department store. Dropping through a skylight, wearing masks and avoiding motion detectors, they lowered themselves to the main hall, broke open display cases, and collected over six million dollars' worth of jewelry. Police investigators found a discarded rubber glove. It had traces of DNA with which they identified twenty-seven-year-old twins with criminal records, Hassan and Abbas O. The twins said nothing, admitted nothing, declined to cooperate in any way. Both were charged and indicted. At the trial, the chief investigator testified that at least one of the brothers was certainly guilty but admitted that the authorities were unable to determine which twin's DNA was on the glove. The court was therefore compelled to release the twins. The third thief was not identified, the loot never recovered.

The Lagnari brothers composed a reply to Justine's attorney and sent a copy to her. In unadorned prose, it stated that they were identical twins, that Justine Kuszalt had willingly slept with both of them on numerous occasions, and that, if pregnancy was the result, a DNA test would not determine paternity. Simon added an unnecessarily brutal sentence: "Moreover, it is not inconceivable that Ms. Kuszalt had other partners during the period in question."

Spencer grunted and gave Simon a fist bump.

A Most Unpleasant Story

Scott and Oswald

A brief fistfight that broke out in the bar of the Drury Plaza Hotel made the evening news in Saint Paul, Minnesota. The story came at the end of the show when viewers are offered a sentimental or humorous item to give the hour of crime and catastrophe the feel of a happy ending. One night, it was the five-year-old who stole the family car and made it to the interstate; the next, a WhatsApp-addicted robber who posted a selfie in his victims' bedroom. Generally, there's nothing amusing about a barfight; but in this one, the combatants were a pair of college professors in town for an academic conference. It was the incongruity of two tweed-clad academics going at it that made the story work, like nuns on Harleys. The story came from an eyewitness's tip, which didn't include an account of the reason for the altercation.

Professors Harold Murphy, 59, and Eugene Horowitz, 31, were in town for a three-day conference devoted to the work of F. Scott Fitzgerald, Saint Paul's pre-eminent native son. Professor Murphy, a distinguished scholar, author of three books and dozens of articles on Fitzgerald and the current editor of *Fitzgerald Studies*, was there to deliver a paper titled "Fitzgerald and History." Horowitz was an assistant professor in his tenure review year. His supportive department chairman arranged for him to be one of two scholars invited to serve as respondents to Murphy's paper. Both were given advance copies of the presentation and asked to respond to it in no more than five minutes.

Murphy's paper included an allusion to "the well-known elements of *Gatsby* inspired by Spengler's *Decline of the West*." The Spenglerian influence on Fitzgerald's masterpiece was ground that had been trodden for decades, often inventively, by many scholars. In fact, the longest chapter in Harold Murphy's career-making first book was an exhaustive treatment of the subject. There was no controversy about the basis of Spengler's influence on *Gatsby*. Authority for it came from the highest source, the author himself. On June 6, 1940, F. Scott Fitzgerald sent a letter to his editor, Maxwell Perkins. In it he wrote, "Did you ever read Spengler?... I read him the same summer I was writing *The Great Gatsby* and I don't think I ever quite recovered from him."

When Murphy finished reading his paper, the first respondent, an associate professor from Notre Dame, author of a book about Zelda Fitzgerald, complimented Murphy's work. She said she was especially obliged for his pointing out the connection between D. H. Lawrence and the visit to the Somme battlefield in *Tender Is the Night*. She then thanked Murphy on behalf of the audience for his many invaluable contributions to Fitzgerald scholarship. Murphy acknowledged her comments with a gratified smile and a collegial nod. The audience applauded politely and began making ready to leave. When Horowitz got to his feet people reluctantly settled down.

"I'm also grateful for Professor Murphy's many contributions and particularly for today's illuminating comments on D. H. Lawrence. But, in the short time allotted me, I would like to say a few words about a more famous influence which he mentioned, that of Spengler on *Gatsby*. While our distinguished speaker was not the first to write on that subject, his first book did the most to establish it as a fixture of Fitzgerald studies. And so, it is with both temerity and compunction that I will be questioning that influence in an article that I will be submitting to the journal so ably edited by Professor Murphy.

"The basis of my disagreement is simply stated. *The Great Gatsby* was published on April 10, 1925. In his letter to Perkins, Fitzgerald said that he was reading Spengler during the summer he worked on the novel, which would have been that of 1924. But Fitzgerald couldn't have been reading Spengler in the summer of 1924 because Charles Francis Atkinson's English translation of Volume One of *The Decline of the West* was published on the first day of January in 1926. Volume Two didn't come out until 1928. It's true that Spengler's two tomes were published in 1918 and 1922, but in German, and Fitzgerald wouldn't have been able to read them."

The room stirred with a rumbling like that of a train slowly approaching a station. Professor Murphy, who had a fair complexion, went briefly pink in the face then he gave out a scoffing guffaw.

"What are you proposing? We have the proof in Fitzgerald letter. Your great discovery is no discovery at all. We all know that Fitzgerald couldn't have been reading *The Decline of the West* while working on *Gatsby*. What he *obviously* meant is that he'd been reading *about* Spengler whose book was making a great stir in the early Twenties. His ideas were in the air. There were slews of magazine articles in English about Spengler and his views. Fitzgerald was referring to those."

Horowitz was shaken, but only briefly. He turned to the senior scholar. "With respect, Professor, Fitzgerald didn't say he was reading *about* Spengler's book but the book itself. He may have read articles, as you say, but I don't know of any hard evidence that he did."

Murphy frowned. Horowitz, daunted and feeling that the ground beneath him was softening, was unwilling to give up his idea. He pushed on by stubbornly defending it at greater length than he'd have preferred.

"Fitzgerald was an alcoholic. He'd been drinking hard for years. His memory might have been unreliable. By 1940, he was in poor health and all but forgotten. *Gatsby* had sold less than 25,000 copies since it appeared fifteen years earlier. He was miserable in Hollywood, unsuccessful as a screen writer, and he'd be dead before the year was out. I think he might have been confused, that his memory was muddled. Spengler did have a big impact on his writing, just not on *Gatsby*. The novel he wrote under the influence of Spengler's ideas is the one that features 'emotional bankruptcy' and examines historical decline from Grant through the Great War and its aftermath. It's the one whose protagonist carries the old ideals but is seduced and tragically falls. It's the book Fitzgerald wrote when both he and the country were suffering from depression. I'm proposing that Spengler didn't influence *Gatsby*—that he couldn't have. However, Spengler's ideas can be found all over *Tender Is the Night*, published in April 1934." Horowitz paused, looked toward the audience then at Professor Murphy. "Thank you all for your attention," he concluded, then. hurriedly returned to his seat.

The restive audience grew noisy and Professor Murphy's face redder. The moderator, a Virginia Woolf expert in a striking red dress, could read a crowd. She strode to the podium and quickly put an end to the proceedings.

Horowitz and his fellow respondent started to come over to shake Professor Murphy's hand, but the professor did not extend his hand to either. He got up, looked disdainfully at Horowitz, stepped down from the dais, and was at once surrounded by a gaggle of admirers.

Professors Murphy and Horowitz had both taken rooms at the Drury Plaza for the weekend. They were staying over for the Sunday luncheon that would conclude the conference. They might not both have chosen to go to the hotel's bar at around five o'clock on Saturday, but they did. Murphy arrived surrounded by old friends and fawning colleagues. They took a booth and ordered a round. Horowitz was on his own. He had never been to a Fitzgerald conference before, knew no one, and nobody was keen to sit with him. He was hoping to do some networking as his chairman advised. He was sitting at the bar sipping the single malt on which he'd splurged when one of Murphy's crowd detached himself and came over to him.

He introduced himself as Nils Anderson from Michigan. "Well," he said, "that was quite something you did today. You didn't make yourself any friends, but it was electrifying. I think Harold was staggered. *I* certainly was."

"I'm sorry to have upset Professor Murphy. I admire him, of course. I just think he was wrong, or rather that he accepted something he ought to have checked. A lot of people did."

Anderson summoned a waitress, and ordered a gin and tonic, then rubbed his chin and suggested that Horowitz might want to apologize to Murphy. "Well, not so much apologize as have a chat about the Spengler business, a friendly one. Murphy has a lot of influence, you know. Might be a wise career move."

Recalling Murphy's dismissive look and red face, Horowitz was reluctant.

"Oh, come on," said Anderson. "He's a good man, bark worse than bite. I'm sure he'll have gotten over the shock by now. He might even call you old sport! Let's go over. I'll come with you."

So, against his better judgment, Horowitz was eventually persuaded to approach Murphy who, by this time, was polishing off his second double Jameson's and had been grousing for half-an-hour about the young moron who had responded to his paper.

As Horowitz and Anderson approached the booth, Murphy's friends fell silent. Anticipating something entertaining, they smiled at each other.

"Professor Murphy," said Horowitz solemnly, "I'm sorry if I offended you this afternoon. If I'd had more time, I'd have been less blunt. I only meant to point out the discrepancy in the dates."

"Only the *dates*, eh?" roared Murphy. "You haven't offended anybody. You've only shown yourself to be unimaginative and pigheaded. You haven't offended me but you have insulted us—both of us. Me *and* Scott!"

Horowitz was taken aback by the vehemence of Murphy's outburst. He took in Murphy's scarlet face and those of the smirking courtiers around him.

"I respect you, Professor Murphy, and I revere Fitzgerald. That doesn't mean you both couldn't make mistakes."

"Oh," said the woman sitting across from Murphy. It was the moderator, still in the red dress.

Horowitz turned toward her. "I once heard a story about a certain sea captain. He was supposed to sail from Lisbon to New York; but, when he left the harbor, he made a half a degree error in setting his course. Confident that he'd gotten it right, he stuck with the heading and didn't check it once during the whole voyage. As a result, he wound up in Brazil."

The woman laughed.

That was when Murphy rose in his seat and, bellowing "Arrogant bastard," threw a pair of wild punches, the only ones of the night. Fending off the blows with his forearm, Horowitz's elbow caught the lurching Murphy's nose, which began to bleed. The men on either side of Murphy grabbed his arms and restrained him as he swore at the younger man and at them.

Horowitz's article was, unsurprisingly, rejected by *Fitzgerald Studies* and then by five other journals. His tenure application was likewise rejected. He spent a couple years as a member of what he called the proletariat of the spirit, cobbling together a living from adjunct and part-time positions. Then he gave up on Academia. With the help of a college friend who had gone into publishing, Horowitz began a new career as a ghost writer, producing marketable autobiographies of garrulous actors, worn-out athletes, retired gangsters, and conceited CEOs.

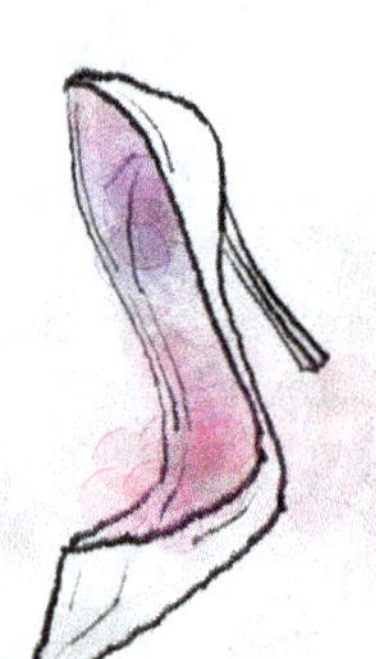

Forgotten Actress

In Grauman's Chinese Theater on March 2, 1944, her twenty-fifth birthday, Jennifer Jones won the Best Actress Oscar for her lead role in *The Song of Bernadette*.

Melanie James, who had turned twenty-six a month earlier, was nominated for her role in the unexpected hit, *The Nightclub Singer*. That she did not win surprised hardly anybody. As one columnist handicapping the awards put it, "Though Miss James' performance was spectacular, she's not just up against the likes of Greer Garson and Ingrid Bergman but also Jennifer Jones and the Blessed Virgin."

Back in 1937, David Rosenfeld, then an unhappy, frequently bullied public school student living in the Bronx, was taken by his Leftist Uncle Morris to see Marc Blitzstein's *The Cradle Will Rock*, directed by Orson Welles. They were lucky to see it, as the production, an amalgam of Broadway musical and Brechtian screed, was shut down the next day by the Works Progress Administration.

David was overwhelmed, star-struck, wowed, changed. He was sure he had found his métier, his vocation, had seen his future. He read Stanislavsky, memorized entire parts from paperback editions of Shakespeare comedies and Gershwin librettos. He auditioned for everything he could and found minor roles in a couple of short-lived off-off-Broadway productions. In 1941, he saw *The Philadelphia Story* and resolved to refocus his ambition from New York to Hollywood. Then came Pearl Harbor and, in February, he received his draft notice. He showed up for induction but, after an interview, was sent home feeling one pound of disappointment, twenty of relief. His parents, who had despaired of him long before, agreed to buy him a one-way ticket to Los Angeles. His mother bagged a lunch for him to take to Penn Station and wrapped a twenty-dollar bill in with a corned beef sandwich. The twenty kept him fed all the way across the country.

David quickly found work in North American's Inglewood plant assembling B-25 bombers, the kind flown by the Doolittle Raiders in their heartening attack on Tokyo. He invested the bulk of his salary in his wardrobe, appearance, and singing lessons. But he went out now and then and, one night in a bar, he was on a stool next to a man who asked if he had any gum. David gave him a stick of Spearmint and they talked. The man extended a big hand. "Joseph MacLaughlin, but everybody calls me Mack." Mack turned out to be an agent. David turned on the charm and only padded his résumé a little. The gent was impressed and not too drunk to do business. He agreed to take David on for ten percent should he get movie work then, as they left the bar, told David he needed a new name and gave him one. Only a week later, Mack called the communal phone in David's apartment building and left an urgent message for him. "Tell him to call me back, pronto."

"Mack? It's David. What's up?"

"Up is right. I've set up a screen test for you at Republic. Next Tuesday, nine o'clock sharp. Talent's getting scarce, I guess. The draft." It wasn't MGM or Paramount, but David was over the moon. To say he passed the test would be putting it mildly and, despite being an unknown, he was offered the part of his dreams.

The film career of Melanie James was truly meteoric: it came out of nowhere, briefly blazed brightly, then was utterly extinguished. It all happened between the fall of 1943 and the spring of 1944. Leggy studio photos of Melanie were pinned up by GIs; her pictures were carefully scissored out of fan magazines by aspiring girls and hormonal boys. Her performance in *The Nightclub Singer*, a steamy blockbuster in which she danced seductively and delivered a practically lascivious rendition of "Makin' Whoopee," was riveting. The film barely adhered to the Production Code and made Melanie famous overnight, a sought-after celebrity and interviewee. When *The Nightclub Singer* made Republic as much money as Warner got from *Casablanca*, the studio made sure their new star was nominated for the Oscar. Melanie yearned to win and her new coterie of sycophants assured her she would, albeit they said something different behind her back.

Jennifer Jones, demurely attired in a dark dress with some faintly sanctified lace at her throat, accepted the Oscar modestly but with obvious pleasure. Despite not winning for her own performance in the title role in *Madame Curie*, Greer Garson made the presentation with grace. Like the winner, she too was discreetly attired and not French.

As the applause died down, Melanie, who was seated next to Marlene Dietrich, got to her feet and headed forward. As the evening's host began to move toward the microphone, she marched up the stairs at stage left and stomped toward a puzzled Jack Benny. There was a collective gasp, some clapping, and an ensign in dress whites stood up and whistled.

Arriving at center stage, Melanie paused to smile at the audience then tore off her wig, undid the top buttons on her blue satin gown, yanked the falsies from her chest and tossed them over her shoulder. When she kicked off her high heels Grauman's fell as silent as the Sanctuary of Lourdes at midnight. David Rosenfeld left the stage in twelve long strides.

Benny crossed his arms and looked sideways at the crowd.

"*Well*," he said. "And I was impressed when Jennifer convinced me she was fourteen, Catholic, and French."

The audience laughed, at first uncertainly then uproariously.

By the next day, both *The Nightclub Singer* and Melanie James had vanished.

Report to the Society

Honored Chairman and Members of the Société d'Exploration Anthropologique, the unrest in S. Province has persisted as long as anyone can remember. The attitude of successive governments to the unrest and sporadic violence in the region can be characterized as indifference at the top and resignation below. The current regime with its progressive agenda would like to pacify and modernize the region. The new First Minister has even made an eloquent and edifying speech to that effect. However, from what I observed, the government is scarcely seen in the interior. The bulk of the province is densely forested; it is far from the capital and, apart from its two population centers, administered in a manner that is little more than nominal. In short, most of the interior along with its denizens remains much as it has probably been for centuries.

Notice the paradox, if you please. While the district is anything but peaceful, it is remarkably stable. I am not exaggerating when I tell you that the region which I visited is in a state of perpetual war; but endless wars, such as the one between the sexes, require, fortunately, innumerable cease-fires. Resentment and hostility are balanced by fascination and need. In such instances, neither adversary seeks the annihilation of the other. Feuds that endure over generations become normal. The conflict furnishes a structure and a culture that infuses life with meaning. As it is with the perennial grievances of men and women, rich and poor, nobles and commoners, the last generation and the next, so it is, ladies and gentlemen, with the Raktan and Nilham of S. Province.

The origin of their conflict can be understood in two ways: ours or theirs. Our way is to look to the economic substructure that drives events. This analysis makes the matter seem as familiar as the quarrel between Cain and Abel, as simple as disputes between ranchers and sodbusters.

The Raktan are patriarchal and live by hunting and fishing while the matriarchal Nilam cultivate crops and raise boars they have managed to domesticate. It is not surprising that each tribe disdains the other's way of life. One would expect the Raktan to see the

Nilam as too settled to be honorable or to view their clearing of land, burning of fields, and diversion of river water as a threat to their fish and game. It is to be expected that in their raids the Raktan would steal the Nilam's pigs, that they would tear up crops, and fill in irrigation ditches.

In the same way, it is understandable that the Nilam regard the Raktan as dirty, uncouth, and bloodthirsty, primitives whose raids threaten their livelihood. So, it is no wonder that they respond with raids of their own, sinking Raktan canoes and extirpating the plants from which their neighbors distill poison for their arrows.

As I say, this is how we would account for the state of war between the two tribes. But remember, this war is perpetual and therefore not total. Raids are always on a small scale, carried out by small bands of young men. Not all Nilam fields are destroyed or all their canals filled in; no more than three or four pigs are ever stolen. Nor have the Raktan, so far as I could discover, ever used their poison arrows against the Nilam. The raiders arm themselves with only cudgels and daggers. The Nilam show a corresponding restraint. At most, only two or three of the Raktan's canoes are staved in, only a few of the curare plants ripped out. The Nilam carry the same weapons as the Raktan, clubs and knives, but neither side seems bent on killing. Victory is defined as a successful punitive expedition, but the victories, like the casualties, are measured by the limited aims. Attacks are intermittent, averaging, I estimate, no more than one every second month.

Before proceeding, I should say a brief word about language. The tribes speak the same tongue; however, there are enough differences to suggest distinct dialects. With your generous support for my expedition, I was able to obtain the services of a translator who knows both dialects, and much else beside. Ms. Ligaya Mahinay is the daughter of a trading family that has been doing business with both tribes since colonial times. She deserves credit for her indispensable contributions to this report.

So, how do the two tribes see things? Not having read Rousseau or Marx, let alone Lévi-Srauss, how do *they* understand the origin of the enmity that defines their lives? They have their own accounts, and these are at the same time contradictory yet consistent. In short, there is one story with two interpretations. The Raktan and Nilam think in tales, the sort we are accustomed to set aside as myths or legends but which they regard as history. I believe that before dismissing such stories we might reflect with some humility on how much of our own history is a patchwork of uncertain stories which, having heard them repeated our whole lives, we unquestioningly take to be factual.

According to both the Raktan and the Nilam, the two tribes once lived if not in harmony, then mostly in peace, sharing a language and worshiping the same animistic deities. Each tribe tolerated the customs if not the dignity of the other. The Raktan may have understood why the Nilam would choose to be governed by a woman, and the Nilam why the Raktan would elect to be led by a man. Why? Simply because the Raktan look down on farming as feminine, just as the Nilam see hunting as crudely masculine. Though there were always disputes between the two groups, even occasional brawls, the vast forest provided for all.

The Nilam and Raktan agree on the event that ended their peaceful coexistence. The feud began when the Nilam queen Tala and the Raktan chief Datu disappeared on the same night, never to be seen again. The Raktan are certain that Tala seduced Datu, cut his throat as he slept, and buried the corpse deep in the forest. The Nilam are equally sure that Datu abducted and raped Tala, then dismembered her body and threw the remains in the river. Thereafter, the two tribes became enemies and to this day young Nilam and Raktan earn their status by raiding. The Raktan carry out daylight attacks, the Nilam nighttime forays. The former honor bravery and power, the latter esteem stealth and cunning. It is hardly necessary to add that each despises the tactics of the other.

The Nilam believe they are avenging their original queen, the Raktan that they are doing the same for their first chief. In this way, a culture arose which, as I said, is at once disordered and disruptive yet stable and structured. As both tribes define themselves through their enmity, neither can do without the other. And so, they have established what I would like to call a symbiosis of war in S. Province, war within narrow parameters, a war both strive to win yet neither wishes to end.

You have been patient, and I promise I am almost finished. There is only one more thing I have to report.

There is a third version of the story of Tala and Datu. This was told to me by my assistant, Ms. Mahinay. One night, as we were reviewing my notes, she said she had remembered something her grandfather told her when she was little. It was a story about a brave chief and a wise queen. She recalled thinking at the time that her grandfather had made up a fairy tale but that, if she remembered correctly, her Lolo claimed he had been told the story by his father who had heard it from an old woman in S. Province. In the story, as she recalled it, the brave chief and the wise queen ruled over different clans who disliked one another, kept their distance, and never intermarried. One day, the chief came to the river to fish and saw the queen who had come to the river to bathe. The chief fell in love with the queen and she, seeing this strong, upright man looking at her longingly, fell in love with him, too. Aware that they could not marry without outraging their people, they resolved to run away and begin a new life together in a distant part of the forest. He would hunt and she would farm, and their children would learn to do both. Ms. Mahinay couldn't recollect whether her grandfather said that the couple lived happily ever after. When I asked, she put her hand to her mouth and laughed.

Of course, ladies and gentlemen, there is no way to know which of the three versions of the story is correct or if all are equally imaginary. And yet, in preparing this report on my expedition, I found myself wishing to believe Ms. Mahinay's grandfather's love story, that it is not a fairy tale but true history while the versions that govern the lives of the Raktan and Nilam are both toxic, self-serving, and destructive misinterpretations.

Thank you once again for your support and thank you as well for your attention this evening.

Failed State

The drug trade in a four-block neighborhood in the northwest of the capital was contested by two gangs, Karum Krew, known as KK, and Shaami Posse Two or SP2. There was little to distinguish the two gangs. Both were made up of adolescents from families the gangs had replaced in their allegiances. Each was led by a man in his twenties with the torso and arms of a weightlifter. KK and SP2 both sourced their merchandise from the same foreign cartel. The boys were semi-disciplined, quick to anger, barely educated, fearless, and street-smart. All were armed with knives or box cutters. Only the muscle-bound leaders and their bodyguards had firearms. Nobody was frightened by the police; rather, it was the police who were afraid of them. The few businesses that had not left or closed down paid protection money to one gang or the other. The largest, an auto and motorbike repair shop, paid both.

After half a dozen youths were killed in eight days, the leaders engaged in a brief effort to negotiate a division of the territory. But diplomacy was not the forte of either, so things went on as before, as tensely but with a bit more restraint. Thanks to the plutocrats in their Mercedes and Range Rovers, from which they never got out, business was brisk and profitable enough. Still, the territory was a mere four blocks and, in the opinion of the SP2's chief, not big enough for both. A merger was out of the question. The two gangs loathed each other, like a brace of jealous fraternal twins.

The chief of SP2, who went by the name of Shredder, was a small-time operator with big-time dreams. What he dreamed of was monopoly and expansion and he knew that the former was a prerequisite of achieving the latter. Once KK had been eliminated, with a base firmly in his hands, he could diversify into prostitution, gambling, kidnapping, loan sharking. He could spread his wings, move into wealthier parts of the city, extort bigger businesses, maybe even arrange phony government contracts. With his narrow, famished eyes, Shredder had been watching gangster films since he was a child, mostly American ones. The American dream meant being a successful crook. When he was starting out, the man who recruited him had a favorite saying: "If you rob a liquor store, you're just a thief; if you steal Asia, you're a god." But to steal well, to flourish, he would need backing. As he saw things, the most efficient way to make himself a bigger tuna was to collaborate with a tuna that was already big.

When Shredder received his monthly delivery in April, he took the courier aside and demanded a face-to-face with a representative of the supplier—"not," he added disdainfully, "some squirt like you but somebody with *juice*. Understand?" When the frightened courier asked why, Shredder smiled contemptuously. "Mutual benefit. Duh," he said, delivering the last syllable like a hammer blow.

A week later, Shredder got a text instructing him to be at the equestrian statue in Central Plaza at precisely four in the afternoon on Monday—and to wear a suit. He borrowed a suit from his skinny cousin. At the appointed time, he was approached in the plaza by a fortyish man in a blue suit that fit. In an accent that was only slightly foreign, he told Shredder to talk fast and not loud.

Shredder offered the Cartel a partnership. With a relatively small investment of cash and muscle, Shredder said the competition could be eliminated and, in due course, he could take over the whole city and organize things properly. He said he had it all worked out. The rise of SP2 would begin with removing the punks of Karum Krew. He asked for help with this first step. Why? Because the boss of KK, called the Hulk, always kept his two toughest men with him, one with a pistol, the other with an Uzi. He thought it imprudent to risk the lives of his boys or, of course, his own. He didn't want any evidence linking SP2 to the operation. "More than plausible deniability," he said, "to keep the cops off our backs."

Shredder was nothing if not thorough. He had two boys watch the Hulk for a month. He knew where he and his top boys hung out and when. They were at the Tugram Bar and Grill every Tuesday and Thursday from noon to three.

The bigwigs of the cartel debated the costs and benefits of using this ambitious Shredder to turn what had been a nose under the tent into a firm foothold, a real beachhead. Some thought it made sense to work with a rising SP2 rather than supplying both them and KK. Small potatoes, they argued. They stood to move more product with an ambitious client who aimed to expand than to go on feeding two small-time gangs who sooner or later would tear each other apart over four miserable city blocks. Those opposed pointed out that if this Shredder was too weak to eliminate the local competition on his own, he certainly couldn't be counted on to expand either his territory or activities. One lieutenant who once had taken an introductory course in economics retorted that they should consider the potential opportunity costs of rejecting the request. Up till now their operations in the capital had been limited. They were mere providers, running a kind of extractive economy. There were riches in that flabby, corrupt capital. Wouldn't it be better to be silent partners? Shredder, he added, had displayed some intelligence in not wanting to attract too much attention to himself, pathetic though the authorities were.

In the end, the big boss decided to oblige Shredder but to minimize the risk of being identified with any violence themselves. "That's bad business," he said. "We can get somebody from the outside. And cheap." Here he turned on the economics expert. "Supply in that segment of the labor force wildly exceeds the demand, no? So, a bus ticket. A hotel room. A few hundred dollars."

The cut-rate contractor the cartel hired was, in some respects, competent. He knew how to smuggle in the components and assemble a bomb. He even understood how to detonate the thing remotely with a cell phone. But he made a vital mistake, if indeed the error was his. Instead of placing the device in the *Tugram Bar and Grill* in the rundown northwest of the city, he planted it in *Restaurant Nubran* in the affluent southwest. It's possible he'd been given the wrong address by his employer. Maybe it hadn't been written down quite legibly. Perhaps he was instructed to memorize the name and did it badly. Impossible to say, as he was murdered three days after using his return bus ticket.

At one o'clock on a Tuesday in May, an explosion tore apart the Nubran, an elegant restaurant popular with ladies from the upper-crust. The blast severely injured seventeen people and blew eight to bits. Among the latter were three toddlers and the pregnant wife of the deputy transport minister.

Disposable adolescents stabbing and shooting one another was deplorable but tolerable. A bomb killing affluent diners and their children two blocks from the National Assembly was not.

From that afternoon events moved at a breathtaking pace. It was as if chaos were a dozing dragon wakened by the blast. The government declared the bombing a terrorist outrage, declared a state of emergency, and deployed troops around the city. The first checkpoints appeared before the sun was down.

On the large military base three miles outside the city, a young colonel convened a secret meeting of junior officers. They had met before, initially airing personal grievances, criticizing senior staff, the ministry, the food. Subsequent sessions were more political. Now the criticism was aimed at the civilians who ran things, the courts, the legislature, the president—all on the take. There were patriotic speeches and pledges of solidarity. The young colonel had laid out his plan for when the time was right. Now, he declared, the time was right. The meeting ended with everyone standing at attention and singing the national anthem.

The coup began at dawn three days after the bombing. Tanks and personnel carriers moved into the capital. The soldiers manning checkpoints mostly joined; the ones who refused were overwhelmed. A few were shot, the others taken into custody. The president fled in a helicopter to an army base in the north. From there he issued a call to the people to defend the constitution and an appeal to all loyal troops to resist the treasonous coup. There were demonstrations in the capital to which the coup leaders responded first with water cannon, then tear gas, and finally live ammunition. Nearly a hundred protestors were killed. In the North, the President rallied his forces, put himself at their head, and began a march on the capital. In the capital, the junta led by the patriotic colonel declared the constitution defunct and the president an enemy of the people.

The bloody civil war was on. Supplies of food, water, and medical equipment began to run out. Looting and banditry spread like cancer. The wealthy raised private militias. Refugees flooded the frontiers of neighboring countries who kept both sides well supplied with weapons but little humanitarian aid. Urgent meetings were convened by the Regional Union and the United Nations Security Council. Resolutions were proposed. The ones that weren't vetoed were ignored.

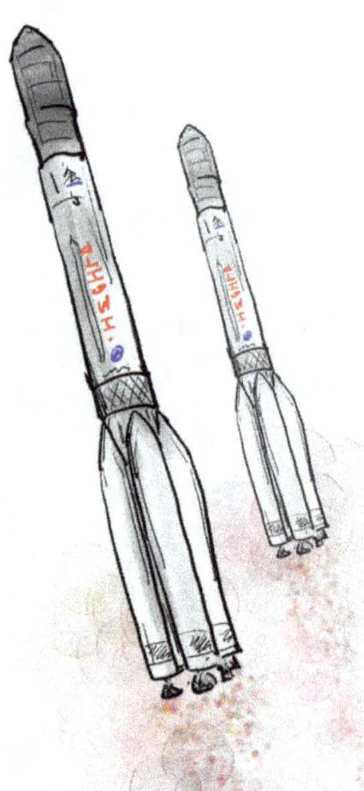

Surprising Consequences of Our Revolution

Like all objects, the object of our revolution was unknowable-in-itself, accessible only through its secondary qualities, its taste, color, odor, texture. Like all revolutionaries, our revolutionary vanguard failed to understand that the object of their sacrifices was unknowable. On the contrary, they passionately believed in the glorious end, not just the taste, color, odor, and texture of the revolution. As we massed on the hills overlooking the spread-eagled capital—literally on the precipice of victory—our leaders smiled at one another. They could smell and touch and taste their final triumph. And it came swiftly, too.

Bottilini, the immensely prolific court composer, died penniless in a gutter at the age of forty-two. In his last appeal to the new Ministry of Culture he had written: "*So I mastered the composition of the string septet. So I wrote over four hundred of the things. Look, I admit the string septet happened to be favored by the Ancien Régime, but is that my fault? Couldn't you people use a few string septets too?*"

The celebrated orator Halbschwacher fell silent. He had been the scourge of the Royalists who had not dared to imprison him for fear that he would convert the other prisoners, the guards, that his eloquence would captivate the very locks. Now that thunderous voice was heard no more. He retired to a cottage on what had once been his country estate, took up bee-keeping and knocking together wooden tables and rush-bottomed chairs. In response to an attempt by the Minister of Propaganda to recruit him, he replied, "*What's there for me to say? You want slogans. Slogans are vulgar. Without the cognoscenti of the Court my talent for invective is obsolete. Best wishes.*"

The revolutionaries now had an inkling that all the consequences of their victory might well have been unknowable and they hastened to fill this intolerable creeping vacuum with ugly apartment blocks, agricultural collectives, hydroelectric dams, steel mills, nuclear reactors, wind tunnels, and rocket engines with enough thrust to launch the Royal Museum into solar orbit. The achievements of their frenzy were amazing. But what of their object, their original goal? Faint traces of its taste, color, odor, and texture may still be discerned from time to time in the swirling, multicolored effluents fouling our rivers.

Pretending is Pretending to Pretend

In 2005, twenty-three-year-old artist Dakota Strether was killed by eight shots fired by two New York City policemen. The meaning of this event was not a matter of dispute. Most New Yorkers were glad about it; the policemen were called heroes, given commendations and two months off. Not a tragedy but a tragedy averted—that was the story, and that was that. But Ms. Strether's friends protested to those who would listen, which was almost nobody, that this bloody business was a terrible misunderstanding. "The masses never get the avant-garde," the painter and songwriter Malcolm Pizzelli, who'd been one of Ms. Strether's five roommates in a SoHo walkup, told the *Village Voice* bitterly. People did want to hear from Dakota Strether's parents, though, but, ashamed and bewildered, the Strethers turned down all requests for interviews, discreetly hauling their daughter's body back to Eau Claire. Besides, what could they possibly say after al-Qaeda declared their daughter a martyr? In a sense, that's just what she was; but the terrorists got it wrong. She wasn't a martyr to their faith, let alone their cause. Instead, Dakota Strether died for a theory.

In what sense theory? One way to put it is to say theory arises when the practical-minded grudgingly grant that some far-fetched eventuality could occur, they say that it might happen theoretically, stressing the third syllable so you'll know what they really think. To many theorists, though—the devoted, the congenital—extremes and improbabilities are irresistible. They will drive their arguments right up to the edge of the cliff then do a swan dive over it. There's a joke about a person of this type who gets elected to the European Parliament. Some obviously level-headed proposal was up for vote, and he rose to object: "I will allow that the plan might work in practice, but—ah—will it work *in theory*?"

The late intellectual Jules Altique, one of the world's most eminent stars a decade ago, was a voluble, prolix, hyperkinetic exponent of theories that were so complex and muffled in language so opaque that even the American graduate students who adored his brilliance couldn't make out what he meant. Altique was so thoroughgoing a theorist that his commitment wasn't to any theory but to Theory itself, to thinking so profound that it transcends the boundaries of physics, our sublunary senses, the human condition. According to his obituary in *Le Figaro*, Altique's politics "appeared to be anarchist, except when they weren't." His cultural tastes, following mysterious strictures, extended from high classical to low popular, as he produced similarly dense essays on Racine, Walt Disney, Catullus, and Madonna.

In his last years, Jules Altique's eminence was nearly as great as Nelson Mandela's. He was the big draw and keynote speaker at the *New York Review of Literature*'s First Conference on Artistic Freedom. It was on this occasion that the great theorist took his most famous position in one of his briefest sentences: "I stand for the liberation of everybody everywhere from everything." It was the first line of his address, as well as his last. In between, he spoke of the obligation to break barriers and challenge limits, to crack the constraints laid like shackles upon human thought and artistic expression. "There is no liberation without transgression," he posited to a crowd of thousands. "All those who seek liberation must have the courage not merely to astonish, to shock, but to outrage, to disgust. I stand for the liberation of everybody everywhere from everything."

Dakota Strether heard Altique's speech; a college friend had gotten her a ticket. When she returned to her friends in SoHo, she was euphoric, inspired. All that gloomy winter she had been stymied by writer's block, painter's block, composer's block, supercharged with the craving to create, yet creating nothing. But now, in her black turtleneck and faded jeans, Dakota announced to her friends that she had at last found her vocation, her purpose. But when they asked what she had in mind, she placed a finger in front of Mona Lisa lips.

A week later, at high noon, Dakota Strether marched resolutely down Broadway in a too-large pea jacket she'd appropriated from Pizzelli. At Chambers Street, she halted by the black iron fence surrounding City Hall Park, doffed the jacket and revealed a fisherman's vest whose pockets she had stuffed with red cylinders and black wires. People looked, made noises, started to run.

"The new always presents itself as atrocious; an authentic artist must not hesitate to appall. Liberation lies in transgression, and all true art is liberating," she wrote in her journal. Dakota Strether looked toward the trees, the fleeing people. Ecstatic about her breakthrough and intoxicated by the verses she was about to declaim, she opened her arms wide. But before she could shout out the first word, the two terrified policemen opened fire.

The Woman in My Bed

A last-minute crisis kept me at work until nearly six o'clock, the hour when I'm accustomed to eating dinner. Before leaving the office, I phoned my local Thai place and ordered Pad See Ew to pick up on the way home. An accident backed traffic up, and by the time I got to the restaurant the noodles were cold. It was that kind of day. Pulling into the driveway felt good; it always does.

During her brief widowhood—before she retired, remarried, moved to Florida, and died—my mother used to complain of having to come home to *a dark cold empty house*. At the time, I was sharing a two-bedroom with slovenly George and punk-rock-besotted Garth. *A dark cold empty house* sounded about ideal to me; it still does. I was raised in a duplex, spent four years in dormitories, then the shared apartment with G and G. I saved up and, when I told my roommates I was going to move out and buy a place, they were sure I'd get a condo in town, "close to work," said George, "near the bars and clubs," said Garth. What I wanted, though, was a place with nobody on the other side of any wall.

I found a just-affordable suburban Cape with a driveway, a magnolia tree, and a hedged-in yard. I planted with Hosta and myrtle and two lignum vitae trees because the garden store expert promised they were fast-growing. The place fitted me like a shortstop's glove, like a mole's burrow.

When I got home with my white box of noodles, I was so famished that I didn't even bother changing into jeans. I switched on the radio, took in the day's bad news, microwaved the noodles, and wolfed them down with a glass of iced tea. Then I went into the living room, flopped on the couch, and flipped on the TV. I was dropping off halfway through an *NCIS* before anybody fired a gun or blew anything up. I decided to make it an early night and plodded upstairs to my bedroom.

A woman was curled up on my bed. She looked a little like an actress I'd seen in an episode of *Midsomer Murders*. She was the second murder victim. Her body had been discovered similarly curled up in the back seat of a Land Rover parked in front of a thatched cottage.

I was on the point of checking for a pulse when I saw that she was taking deep, even breaths. Relieved, I stepped back from the bed. The woman's mouth was slightly open, showing white teeth and the tip of a pink tongue. My mattress is a full, wider than a twin, narrower than a queen. She was lying near the edge of the bed, as if leaving space for me. She raised a shoulder, drew up her knees, and made a noise like the sigh of someone who needed a back rub and was getting it.

I yawned. Should I wake her? I decided against it.

My little house had a small second bedroom with my old twin mattress on the floor. It had only been used once, when my nephew broke up a trip to New York by spending the night.

I took sheets and pillowcases from the linen closet as quietly as I could.

In the office, phones were always ringing or playing ring tones; there were informal greetings, bad jokes, sports talk, pinging emails, gossip to be whispered. I liked the silence of my snug home. In the small bedroom the quiet felt denser, as if it had been compressed. I tiptoed into the bathroom, took off my clothes, brushed my teeth as soundlessly as I could, slipped into the bedroom, shut the door, made up the bed, and tried not to think about the woman in my bed. I wanted to sleep and wondered if she would be gone in the morning.

I lay on my back and shut my eyes, but the drowsiness was evaporating. The house was quiet but the silence felt precarious. Despite myself, I listened hard. I hadn't seen any clothes on the floor of my bedroom. The woman in my bed must be clothed.

I put my hands behind my head and reviewed my relationships with women. All but the last had ended quickly, by mutual consent and without drama. The last had lasted almost two years and ended badly, which perhaps was why it was the last. I had broken it off without meaning to, without premeditation, seemingly on impulse. The words escaped me before I could call them back. The woman was married; I had no idea how happily because she never mentioned her husband's name or talked about her marriage. Sometimes I thought her silence was meant to spare me, at others that she was roping me off. I sometimes felt that I only existed for her when we were together, in those golden, stolen afternoons, while I thought of her all the time. Did she love her husband? Me? Both of us or neither? To ask would be a risk, the violation of a tacit contract. We could talk about anything—politics, books, work, movies, our childhoods, history, theology, technology, the national debt—but never the essential thing. This relationship was a secret that made the two of us a secret. So our bond was intimate but at the same time inconsequential. The agreement worked until the moment it didn't, the moment I opened my mouth and blew it to smithereens. I thought I had acted on impulse, a moment of resentment of coming last on her list of priorities; but that night I realized that I had felt humiliated because my half of the emotional scale outweighed hers. It happened all at once. She phoned to cancel lunch, I asked why. Wasn't she free? Her answer was two full seconds of silence, two decisive seconds. The hiatus could have meant a lot of things, but to me it signified to me one thing. "Nothing," I found myself saying, "nothing is better than this." The sentence burst from me like a cough, a sneeze. Nothing is better than this. The words were the very ones I had whispered into her ear the first time we'd gone to bed together. Nothing is better than *this* twisted into *Nothing* is better than this.

Happiness makes us vulnerable; love makes it worse. I took that nothing to heart and killed off the instinct for something. I chose the harmless pleasures of books, music, movies, gardening, solitary biking. I puttered proprietarily around my house, pleased as ever that nobody else was on either side of its walls.

I got up, went to look. The woman in my bed was dreaming; her eyes moved under their lids. What could she be dreaming of? Surely not of being where she was. She must have gotten into the house while I was at work, Goldilocks sneaking into the bears' snug den. It seemed imperative not to wake her. I noticed her left ear beneath a swirl of dark hair. It was a small and perfectly formed ear, like a child's. Her cheek was as smooth as an infant's, too. In fact, looking down on her in the moonlight coming through the window, I felt like a father checking on his little girl, assuring himself that she was sleeping comfortably, prepared to do mortal battle with anyone who threatened her.

I looked again for her clothing, but there were no clothes, no shoes either. Could she have put her things away in my dresser, hung them in my closet? It seemed improbable. If she'd arrived naked had she been stripped, fleeing from an attacker? Had she escaped from him and run to my house, tried the door and found it unlocked? But I was always careful about the locks.

I went down to the kitchen and turned on the light. I checked to see if the back door had been forced or a window broken. The house was tight as a safe-deposit box or a coffin. Of course, it was possible that for once I had left something open, that she had made her way in and locked up behind her. If she had been fleeing an attacker, she would certainly have done that.

I tiptoed back up to my bedroom. She had moved. Now she was stretched out on her right side, two pillows under her head, the duvet pushed down. Her left shoulder and one breast were exposed, and I gently pulled the duvet back over her. Stepping quietly to the closet, I opened the door slowly, took my bathrobe from its hook, and laid it on the floor beside the bed so she would have something to put on when she woke up. Then I went back to my exile in the small room with the small mattress.

Near morning, I finally fell into a fitful sleep but that ended when the sun came up. I was briefly disoriented, surprised to find myself where I was. My watch was still on my wrist, and I saw that it was only a few minutes after six, forty-five minutes before I usually got up to go to work. My clock-radio was in the other room, but I hadn't set the alarm.

I got up, put on my clothes, and tried to think of what I would say to her when she woke. The phrase "home invasion" came into my head trailing images of thugs in black balaclavas wielding big kitchen knives, interlopers destroying the inviolability of my haven. I almost chuckled. In the next room was a naked, helpless, vulnerable woman. She was at my mercy.

I imagined a domestic scene in the kitchen. I would make coffee. The aroma would wake her and she would come downstairs in my robe. Would she like a bagel with raisin bran or prefer eggs and toast with strawberry jam? Tea or coffee?

I checked my watch again. I had to be on the road before seven-thirty. I sat down at the kitchen table and focused my mind on the draft of the report I had left unfinished on my desk. I thought of an idea I could add, some better-turned phrases. It was an important report, the fruit of a month's work, the only item on the agenda of the big Friday meeting.

Nature called. I went to the downstairs bathroom. It was almost seven o'clock. Time to act. I went back upstairs, not on tiptoes this time.

Sunlight streamed in. My robe had vanished. The bed was empty. The two pillows were fluffed and set neatly side by side. The duvet was pulled tight.

I rushed back downstairs, dashed through the vacant living room and hurried to the kitchen. It was empty too but there was a piece of paper in the middle of the table, torn from the pad I kept by the phone. In a rounded feminine hand was a short message. "Better this way. I'll put the robe in the mail."

The Woman in My Bed

Grandfather's Dao

Josh and I were usually careful; nevertheless, in our senior year I got pregnant. We'd been a couple since locking eyes as sophomores, so, after the panic evaporated, we decided to get married. Our parents weren't pleased. We'd have been content with a Justice of the Peace and a pair of witnesses dragged off the street, but my grandfather insisted on footing the bill for a big shindig. "If it's a mistake," he wrote in a letter I've laminated, "I'd like it to be a spectacular one. And, my dear, if it's not a wrong turn, so much the better."

After I miscarried, we found we had made a grievous goof. Three days after the divorce came through, my grandfather, who had by then been diagnosed, sent me a puzzling present. It arrived in a long cherrywood box nestled in shavings that smelled fresh. There was a card: "With lots of love from Opa."

It has three wings, impractical, asymmetrical. Two are dazzling under the light, like kaleidoscopes filled with luminous anemones. The other is a dull tan or beige and thicker than the others. The matched pair are graceful and elliptical, like Spitfire wings, the other looks a little like a rough model of a surfboard made by some precocious child. Running down the length of the object is a metal armature. It's a dull silver, like an old ladle a day before the butler's assistant does the polishing. At first, I thought it was a simple, smooth oblong, but then I noticed it had a slight concave curve to it and, under the magnifying glass, elaborate chasing, what looked like fleurs-de-lis and laurel leaves, something classical, maybe Florentine. The two spiral extensions on either side were like riddles asking to be solved and sure you'd fail. Assuming they had one, they kept their purpose between themselves, like a pair of playful, twirling dolphins. When I turned the object over, I found it had five tiny wheels, retracted like landing gear waiting for a runway. At one end there are a pair of small, round rubies that made me think of the eyes of some underpaid copyeditor working on an edition of *Das Kapital* in 8-point Gothic font. Four hand-like protuberances have four digits each, a thumb and three fingers. The latter are white, the former green. I thought of Mickey Mouse as a gardener who'd had a couple of accidents with a hedge-trimmer. On the top, just above the ruby-eyes, is a button. When I tried pushing it a recording spoke, but in such a little voice that I had to listen five times before I could barely make it out. It sounded like "You change, you who." But when I tried again later it was more like "You change you woo."

I showed the object to a few friends, including Chen Mailing. When I pushed the button and asked her to put her ear close, she laughed.

"It's not *you change*," she said. "It's *Yu cheng yu wu*."

"What?"

"*Yu cheng yu wu*. It's from Laozi. Ancient Chinese sage."

"What does it mean?"

"Being comes out of non-being."

The Theoretical Ship

Dittlos was up with the sun, squinting at the waves sparkling merrily. The fishermen were either preparing their boats or already pushing off. In a few hours the procession of the chosen fourteen would arrive with the priests and priestesses, flute-players and thieves, the whole urban mob pouring down from the city ready for the annual holiday. He had put off what he had to do until the last moment. Why did he dread what was his duty, his destiny—and not just his, but his father's and his father's before him, going back five generations. Dittlos' father had predicted this day after making the last of his entries on the family's scroll, the record of their repairs. Pistos had said to twelve-year-old Dittlos, "If the gods spare you, son, the last plank will be laid by you."

Weeks ago, after he pushed his thumb deep into the spongy plank, he had cut the replacement to length and smoothed it. Then he put it aside. Did he expect the rotten plank would be made miraculously sound, that Apollo or Poseidon would see to it? Not at all. Dittlos felt the full force of what he had to do and the confusion it could excite. Should he tell anybody? And what did he, Dittlos, think? He had a long time to ponder the question, but he was still of two minds. But then so much about Theseus himself was ambiguous. For instance, Dittlos had heard a few old men claim that the hero founded Athens, while most others scoffed pointing out that he was the son of Aegeus, who was king of Athens. Theseus could hardly be the founder of a city of which his father was already king. The ambiguity of Theseus began in the womb. His mother Aethra, wife of Aegeus, was said to have been impregnated by Poseidon, in which case he wasn't the proper heir of Aegeus. Others say that he was Aegeus' son, and that the Poseidon story was just the Greeks' custom of turning a hero into a demigod. Demigod? Isn't that ambiguous too, thought Dittlos. Theseus raised the rock, retrieved Aegeus' sandals and sword, was acknowledged by the king, and claimed his patrimony. But what was it Aegeus' acknowledged, that Theseus was his son and heir or that the boy had passed a test any muscular adolescent might have, especially if he were the son of the sea god?

Minos and Ariadne, the dispatching of the Minotaur, rescuing of the seven boys and seven girls, and the other adventures of Theseus culminated in his uniting of the demes in the *Synoikismos*, all of which was embodied in the ship, Athens' ship of state. And all of it was commemorated in the annual voyage to Delos to honor Apollo with the chosen fourteen. For this, the city purified itself, suspending executions, with lustrations and better behavior. The ship had therefore to be maintained and it was to the family of Dittlos that the task had been assigned generations ago.

But when the last plank was replaced—what then?

The ship of Theseus would no longer be Theseus' ship, thought Dittlos. But then he asked why were the hull, the planks, the ropes, and oars significant? Wasn't it because of what they represented, what people thought of when they saw them? The ship was as ambiguous as Theseus' paternity, both a thing and an idea. An idea is more durable than wood that rots, more powerful because immutable. After all, the chosen boys and girls who would shortly be boarding were not the sacrifices sent to Crete. Nor was Dittlos any longer the boy who had heard Pistos' prediction. What did it matter if the ship was not the original one? And yet, it did matter. And wasn't the twelve-year-old Dittlos somewhere inside the forty-year-old carpenter?

Theseus unified Attica. He saved seven boys and seven girls to help populate it. Should the Athenians learn that not even a single splinter of his original ship was left, they would, being Athenians, divide into camps and start to debate. The argument could turn bitter and undo the work of Theseus.

Dittlos fitted the final plank to the deck and then, instead of recording what he had done, he burned the family scroll. But he was unable to keep anything from his faithful wife Noikia. Nor could Noikia keep anything from her dearest friend Kalytera.

The End of the War

By the ninth year we believed it might never end and gave up trying to win it because trying to win a war is the surest way to make it go on; that is, when you try to win a war it's only the war that wins. This was the sum of the wisdom we had achieved in nearly a decade; in fact, it was the solitary thing we had achieved in all those years of fighting and suffering. Now that we were pushing thirty, we couldn't bear that the war would go on and on, not just for another decade but for the rest of our lives. Nevertheless, simply laying down our arms and surrendering would be futile because of the swarms of gung-ho seventeen- and eighteen-year-olds, weaned on tales of glory and revenge, who wouldn't think of giving up, at least not for another nine more years. As for ourselves, our generation, we reckoned that it wasn't the enemy that needed to be defeated but the war itself. It had already ruined everything it touched, from dairy farms to post-adolescence, from stone bridges to summer romances, from highway overpasses to bedside manners, from the pride of old men to the breasts of pubescent girls. So, by and by, we came up with a plan, desperate yet not inelegant. A dozen of us decided to organize a theater festival, as we announced, *right on the front lines* (of which there really weren't any), *right in the middle of the battlefield* (though there really was no field). Our great production would stretch from the trenches to the rear echelons, from the barracks all the way to the field kitchens and mobile hospitals. We persuaded ourselves that in this way we might bamboozle the war into thinking it wasn't a real war at all but only make-pretend. Our theatrics would confuse the generals, baffle the colonels, mystify the majors, deceive even the sergeants (who are always the most difficult to fool). We would make them believe they were not combatants at all but directors, stagehands, managers, grips, prop men, script girls, even, in the case of the elderly and august field marshal who headed the General Staff, a playwright. When the last scene of the final act was played, we would invite the international press and hand out awards. Critics from all the papers and television networks, bored with repeating patently false government communiqués, would be eager for the novelty of the business, and also frightened of missing something so unheard-of, so *avant-garde*, that they would flock to our vast theater. We would work the artillery barrages into the script, and the nighttime bombings as well. The streams of refugees would serve as extras in our epic production. We would take pains that even the smallest skirmish was properly lit, that there would be plenty of applause for heroes who acted persuasively heroic and no less for cowards capable of acting convincingly craven. If the cowards should turn out to be the more persuasive, then the cowards would receive the acting award and not the heroes. And soon, the war would forget its intention to be endless; it would be gobbled up by the glory of art as, under our high-school microscopes, we'd watched a paramecium ingest some morsel that became a piece of satisfied paramecium paddling purposefully through its little world. In this way, so we thought, the war too would gradually cease to be itself and become the subject of our vast theater-piece complete with its rising action, its recognition, reversal, and climax, with its rapidly falling action concluding in a most delicious dénouement where each enmity and conflict would be unknotted and made smooth, when all the terrible energies of our sanguinary youth would at last come to rest. The audience of millions would feel this approaching closure like a train rumbling toward the platform and this rumbling, this muted expectancy would be satisfied even if one didn't particularly care for the play (it's true that most people don't like most plays) because everyone would know that soon they would be permitted to rise from their narrow seats (there is never enough leg room for those who have legs), released and granted all the time they wanted to mull over the faults of the drama in a café, then to make their way home, climb between clean sheets, and forget all about it.

Haran

Their jagged laughter still tearing at his ears, Abram crouched as if beaten and entered the cool entry of his brick house. In an inner chamber Sarai was berating the cook, or perhaps it was one of the maids this time. The men's laughter had evaporated quickly. The bleating of a single ram rose into the hot afternoon. Abram sat down and pressed his back against the wall.

So, every one of them had also heard the voice, had likewise received some colossal promise. "Oh, sure, sure," they had said with derisive smiles. And one: "I myself had much the same hallucination years ago. You're a stranger here; listen to me. Mirages and delusions like yours are common hereabouts, especially up in the hill country during the long summers. But to leave our rich fields and our fine pastures, these decent houses and good wells? Leave all this for the barbarous wastes down south? It's a completely ludicrous notion; get hold of yourself man. Think of your wife."

Every one of them had been cured—one by sleep, one by lying with his wife, another by an emetic.

A Note on the Type

This book is set in Alda, a typeface designed by Berton Hasebe for the Emigre type foundry in 2008.

The inspiration for Alda came from Berton's explorations of generating different type weights by adapting the characteristics of physical objects: the boldest weight as tense as bent steel—the lightest as floppy as a rubber band. One unreleased weight was purportedly based on the squishiness of a housecat, and was an utter failure.